Other books by Bobbie Montgomery:

Keeping Daddy Single
Three Blondes in a Honda
Fruit Tramp Kids

Visit our website at *www.rhpa.org* for information on other Review and Herald products.

Bobbie Montgomery

REVIEW AND HERALD® PUBLISHING ASSOCIATION
HAGERSTOWN, MD 21740

The author assumes full responsibility for the accuracy of all facts
and quotations as cited in this book.

Interior design by Bill Kirstein
Cover design by Genesis Design
Cover illustration by Kim Justinen
Typeset: 11/15 Veljovic

PRINTED IN U.S.A.

03 02 01 00 99   5 4 3 2 1

R&H Cataloging Service
Montgomery, Bobbie, 1918-
    Donkey-cart kids.

        1. Title

                813.54

ISBN 0-8280-1442-6

Dedication

To my mother, Vickie Dear,
who has always encouraged
me never to give up.

Chapter One

"Help! Help!" Linda screamed. "Nanny Goat's running away with the tickets. Michael! Help me!"

Her brother came running around the house. "What's going on?"

"Catch Nanny! She has the train tickets," Linda yelled again as she raced after the goat, who bounded through tall, dry grass, a yellow paper waving in her mouth.

Michael darted past Linda after the animal. Nanny Goat glanced over her shoulder.

"Nanny, get that gleam out of your eye," Michael hollered. "Stop. Stop!"

"Wait for David and me," Joe shouted from the old orchard. Red, their big dog, barked behind the twins as they tried to catch up with Michael and Linda.

Little Betty stood in the doorway of the house, pulling on one of her long curls, repeating over and over, "Nanny's got the train tickets. Nanny's got the train tickets." Then she shouted, "I'll help too," and started after the others.

Catching up with Nanny, Michael grabbed her collar. The goat shook her head, gave a last crunch on the yellow paper in her mouth, and swallowed it. The children gathered around the goat, staring in horror while the animal blinked her eyes and switched her tail.

"What will we do?" Linda moaned. "She's eaten the train tickets."

No one bothered to answer.

Nanny started walking away. "No! You don't get away!" Michael stormed. He grabbed the goat around the neck with one arm, pried her mouth open, and peered down her throat.

"Do you see anything?" Joe asked.

"Just her tonsils," Michael muttered, glaring at Linda. "Leave it to a girl. How did it happen anyway?"

Betty put her hand in Linda's and the girls sank down in the grass. Then Linda explained. "We were sitting on the porch. Betty wondered if we were really going to Grandma Bell's farm to live. I got the tickets to prove we were. Betty counted each one and wanted to pull them apart. I told her one might get lost if they were separated. That's when Nanny grabbed them. What will we do?"

"I don't know," Michael grumbled. "I could hitchhike 85 miles but not with a bunch of little kids."

"You wouldn't leave us," Joe stated.

"Of course not," Michael answered, staring off in the distance.

Ever since their dad had died, Mom had been sick. The children tried to help by following her directions. Michael was 12. Mom called him the head of the family. He did all the business, shopping, and heavy work around the home. Linda, 11, did the cooking, while Mom supervised from the bedroom. Linda also took care of 5-year-old Betty and kept their clothes washed. The twins, Joe

8

and David, though only 7, did their share. All worked together without much fussing.

Mom said they were the best kids ever—most of the time.

She had Michael sell many of their things to obtain money for the bills, but there wasn't enough for house payments.

Uncle Cecil offered to help, but he worried Mom. He wanted to adopt the children. When Mom refused, he became angry and threatened to tell the police she couldn't handle them.

After his last visit she said, "Michael, it's your job to keep the children away from Cecil. He's not a good man. I love my sister, but Cecil drinks and uses bad language. Whatever happens, stay away from him. Never take his help! Promise!"

"I promise," her son said firmly.

Three days before, Mr. Smith, one of the neighbors, had moved their few belongings and animals to this old place. It was lonely away from everyone, but it was fun exploring new territory.

Yesterday their mother had gotten very sick, and Michael had the doctor come. "Lady, if you want to get well," the doctor said seriously, "you'll stay in a sanitarium at least a year. Is there someone to take your children?"

Faintly she answered, "Their father's mother, but I can't afford a sanitarium."

"Don't you worry about the expenses. That will be taken care of, and you can think about it when you get well. See about your children, and I'll make the arrangements." Then he left.

Mom knew she must go. That morning she had sent

Michael with all their money after the train tickets for their trip to Grandma Bell's. Before he left, he called Mr. Smith for advice about where to leave the animals, but no one answered.

Just as he opened the door after his walk from town, the ambulance came for Mom. "It's here," she said sadly. "The doctor sent it."

He squeezed her hand.

"Did you have enough money for the tickets?" She asked quickly.

"Yes, and a dollar left."

"Michael, call Grandma collect and tell her you're coming. You must go on the very next train. Uncle Cecil is apt to find where we've moved. It's possible you couldn't cope with him."

"I will, Mom."

With worry in her eyes, she kissed each one good-bye. "Be good Christians. Remember your best friend is Jesus. Grandma will be happy to have you. Be a help to her. It won't be long until we're together again."

The little ones started crying when the ambulance sped down the road. To keep from crying himself, Michael growled, "Be quiet. We have to pack. Besides, now I remember that the Smiths started their vacation today. That's why they didn't answer the phone. We have a problem to figure out. What shall we do with the animals?"

Now, several hours later, Michael straightened his shoulders. No use going over all their bad times. Nanny had stirred up a new problem for them: How would they get to their grandmother's without tickets?

"Maybe we can sell Nanny," Joe suggested.

"We can't get five train tickets for her. Any suggestions, Linda?"

The girl didn't answer.

"We can't fly," Joe laughed.

"We can't ride the bus either," David added. "Everything costs money, if you don't have tickets."

"Guess we'll have to ride Jake," Betty piped up, shaking her yellow curls. "That won't cost anything."

Michael laughed at the idea of all five kids climbing on their little donkey's back and traveling 85 miles to Grandma Bell's farm. Jake hee-hawed from the old orchard as if voicing his opinion about that.

The younger children ran to play with the little donkey, leaving Linda and Michael to worry alone.

He saw his sister brush tears from her face. "Aw, quit crying, Linda. You didn't do it on purpose. Nanny Goat's money hungry."

Linda laughed shakily and watched the twins push a two-wheeled cart behind Jake. Betty held the donkey's halter. The animal snorted and pulled away from her.

"You guys will have to help," Joe yelled at Linda and Michael.

They joined the others and hitched Jake up to the cart. "What are you playing?" Linda asked.

"We're not playing," Joe answered. "We're helping get ready for the trip to Grandma's."

"You're crazy!" Michael exclaimed.

Ignoring the remark, Joe continued, "We'll be pioneers. This is our covered wagon, only it isn't covered."

Linda's eyes began to dance with excitement. She jumped up and down, exclaiming, "Michael, they're right!

Everybody walked in pioneer days. It isn't far. Think how long the Oregon Trail was. The pioneers took cows on their journey. We'll take Nanny along, and she'll give us milk. We can camp at night."

Michael looked at his sister in disbelief. "You mean it, don't you?"

"Of course I mean it. There isn't any other way."

"Somebody'd stop us."

"Who? Smiths won't be home for two weeks. The rent's paid. The owner won't be around for a long time."

"Well," Michael answered slowly, "there are the neighbors."

"They live a long way off," Joe volunteered.

"Besides, we don't know them, and they don't know us."

"We won't tell anybody about it," Linda planned out loud. "We can't worry Mom—she's too sick. Grandma doesn't know we're coming, unless you want to ask her for money, or we could see if the neighbors will help. Do you want to do that?"

"Don't be silly. Mom always said, 'Take care of your own problems. Don't bother other folks.' We can figure this out ourselves."

"OK," Linda ordered. "Quit stalling. We'll take blankets."

"Just a minute, Linda! Are you bossing me? It's dumb, and you know it."

"It's dumb to stay here until Uncle Cecil comes," she retorted.

Michael grew thoughtful. After a while he laughed, "Why not? That will take care of the animals and Uncle Cecil too. OK, let's walk. We've got to leave now before Uncle Cecil finds out anything. If we wait, we're lost."

"Get busy, boys," he ordered. "Pick a pail of apples and put them in the cart. Linda, you get food and blankets. Betty, help Linda. I'll do the rest."

The twins gave a wild yip as they grabbed a pail off the porch and ran to the orchard.

Michael searched through some boxes for their little ax. He could hear Linda talking to Betty. "We'll take the frying pan and the red kettle, these old tin cups and plates, and the white bucket for milk and water."

Linda put the things in a box, and Michael carried it out to the cart. When he returned, Linda pointed to each article in another box. "There's macaroni, dry beans, five potatoes, two cans of corn, a tiny bit of oil, a little flour, sugar, and a box of salt. Not much, but we'll have milk. I put Mom's sewing box in too. Something might come apart."

"OK, I'll get a rope. It might be handy."

Linda shrugged. "This little bag has the soap and towels in it. We have to keep clean. Here are clean clothes in a flour sack."

"A blanket for each of us is enough. August is hot," Michael muttered as he loaded the cart.

She piled a white cotton blanket on top. "That's a spare."

Betty and Linda put everyone's coat in the cart. "We can use them for pillows at night," Linda explained.

Locking the house, Michael put the key into his pocket. "Guess we're all ready," he announced. "We have a right to leave our stuff here. Mom said that after the busy season Grandma'd probably come after it."

"Michael, are you scairt?" Linda asked.

"Forget it. Everything's ready. Nanny's tied to the

back of the cart. Red always stays with us. No use tying a good dog like him."

"Where's Goldie?" Betty inquired. "Oh, she's around somewhere," Michael replied.

"Where will she ride?"

"Goldie can't go," Linda replied. "It would look silly to take a hen traveling. She can eat grass and bugs around here."

The little girl's face grew stern. "We can't leave her here. She'd get lonesome without me. I'm going to stay with Goldie. If Goldie can't go, I can't go."

"It wouldn't look any sillier for a banty hen to go traveling than a goat, a dog, and a donkey," Joe argued.

"She sits on Jake's back," David added. "She could ride there."

"Eggs are good to eat," Betty said firmly. "Goldie could lay her eggs in the cart."

"It's a good thing Mom sold Nanny's kids, or you'd want them along, and I think it's just as bad to take a chicken," Michael persisted. Linda looked reproachfully at her brother. "Of course Linda eventually wants what Betty wants," he fumed to himself. "Goldie'll be trouble, even if we do love her. Take her," he said out loud. "But don't expect me to hunt for her when she gets lost."

The twins ran toward the old barn and soon returned with the hen. Betty took the chicken in her arms. "Don't you worry, Goldie," she soothed.

"We will tell no lies," Michael instructed the children. "That's one of the important things Mom taught us. We can be careful, though—we won't tell people all our business. If anyone asks where we're going, we'll just say, 'To our grandma's.' That's the truth. Don't tell anyone how far we're going. We'll just say, 'Down the road.' Better not talk much."

He glanced at the watch Mr. Smith had given him for Christmas. "It's 10 minutes till two. We'll hurry until we get to the other side of Lakeview."

"Come on, Red," Linda called to the big hound dog as they started.

"Let's go, Jake," Michael yelled at the donkey. Nanny followed behind the cart, and Red dashed ahead as they went down the road.

Later, as they approached Lakeview, Michael decided to go around the edge of town and take a gravel road. "It's farther, but we can't go where there will be many cars. Somebody might get wise," he explained.

"Besides," Linda added, "this road goes along the beach later. That will be fun."

The twins and Red ran ahead of the others, investigating small holes in the ground. Linda untied the goat's rope from the cart and led her along the edge of the road so she could nibble choice clumps of grass.

It was hot, and Jake wouldn't hurry. He seemed to have strict rules about never going faster than an amble.

They hadn't gone far on the old road when a patrolman stopped his car beside Michael and the cart. "That's quite a donkey you have there," he commented.

"Yes," Michael replied, pulling on Jake's reins. "But he's slow."

"Would you like to see Goldie?" Betty asked from her place in front of the cart. She held the little banty hen up in the air. "Pretty soon she's going to lay an egg. We might have it for dinner."

The officer looked interested and climbed out of his car. "Where will she lay the egg?" He asked.

"Maybe in my lap, because I have to watch her. Michael won't hunt for her if she runs away. I want Grandma to see Goldie."

The patrolman laughed and patted Betty's golden curls. Then he turned to Linda. "Are you going to show the goat to Grandma?"

She nodded.

Just then Red and the twins came bounding back. "Hurry up, Michael," Joe yelled. "We're hungry."

"Besides, we'll never get to Grandma's the way you're poking around," David added.

The boys grew quiet when they saw the patrolman.

Michael took a firmer grip on Jake's reins as his thoughts whirled. "The officer will ask how far we're going. Then he will ask more questions. He will tell Mom or Grandma what we're doing. Everybody will get worried, and Mom will get worse. Some head of the family I am!"

The officer inspected the cart. "Which way are you going?"

Michael pointed. "We're following this old road to the right."

Betty smiled at the officer. "We've got things to eat. It's a picnic. When we get up the road, Michael says we can eat. Would you like to eat with us?"

"No, little girl, I can't eat with you. I'm on my way to work. But I'll tell you what I will do. I'll fix that hen of yours so she can't run away."

Drawing a long piece of string from the glove compartment of his car, he made a noose at one end. He slipped the noose around one of Goldie's legs and tightened it. Then he handed the string to Betty. "There, little girl. You won't lose your pet."

Turning to Michael and Linda, he said, "You kids stay on the left side of the road and watch for cars. Be careful! Your Grandma wants to see you in one piece." Smiling, he got in his car and waved to them as he turned around and drove away.

Betty climbed out of the cart with Goldie. She put the hen on the ground, holding tight to the string. "Wasn't he a nice policeman to fix Goldie for me?" She asked happily.

Linda looked at Michael, and they sighed together in relief. "Well, we got by," Linda said. "We better hurry up before he decides to come back and find out where Grandma lives."

"Yes, we got by this time," her brother replied. "I didn't know policemen were so friendly and helpful. They'll be stopping us all the way. Somebody's going to let the whole thing out. Then we'll be in trouble for sure."

Chapter Two

As they looked for a place to eat along the old road, Linda complained, "There doesn't seem to be a real picnic spot."

"No," Michael answered, "just fields and fences."

"I don't care whether it's a picnic spot or not," Joe said. "I can eat anywhere. I'm hungry. David's hungry too. We didn't have any lunch, you know."

"See that oak tree up the road?" Michael pointed. "It's about the best place. It seems to be past the fenced-in fields."

"We'll have to walk quite a way to get there," Linda said. "Oh, well, let's hurry. It won't take long."

They plodded along, trying to get Jake to move a little faster, but he had his own ideas about speed.

"At last," Michael sighed as he halted Jake under the tree. "Not much grass for Jake and Nanny, and no water."

"Michael, make a fire, and we'll heat the corn in the cans," Linda directed. "We'll have bread and corn, with apples for dessert. Betty, give Nanny and Jake an apple. That will be their drink of water until we come to a creek."

Her brother scooped dead leaves into a little pile and put dry twigs from the tree on top of them. Then he lit a match to the leaves. It was a tiny fire but hot.

"I'm glad we have a can opener," Linda commented as she opened the cans of corn and placed them straight on the twigs. In a short time the corn was bubbling hot. While Linda filled each plate, Michael covered the little fire with dirt to keep it from starting a blaze later.

All of them sat quietly under the oak tree eating their lunch. Jake and Nanny nibbled at small patches of dry grass. Goldie pecked at grasshoppers. Red sat on his haunches with his long tongue lolling out of his mouth, waiting for his share.

As they munched on their apples, Linda said, "Everybody wipe their own dishes out with leaves. We'll wash them tonight. No water here."

"It's hot. Even Betty better walk," Michael said as he loaded the grocery box in the cart again. "We don't want Jake to get tired."

"We sure don't," David laughed. "When Jake gets tired he balks."

Betty tied the hen's string to one of the coats in the cart, and they started their journey. They hadn't gone far when Goldie said, "Ca-ca-ca-ca-dak-a."

Betty ran to the cart. "Goldie's laid an egg! Goldie's laid an egg right in the corner of the cart! Nice Goldie!"

Linda took the egg and wrapped it in leaves so it wouldn't get broken, then she put it inside one of the tin cups. "You were right, Betty. We need Goldie. Now we'll have pudding. Mom taught me how to make pudding out of flour, egg, and sugar. I'm trying to do like Mom. I'm the mother until she gets well and comes to Grandma's."

"You're a good mother, Linda. I love you," Betty said, wrapping her fat little arms around her sister.

David and Joe raced back and forth with Red.

"Stop running!" Michael ordered. "Just walk with the rest of us. You'll be tired before evening."

"We'll never get tired," Joe argued. "We're big, strong twins. We can go forever."

"That's what you think."

It wasn't long until David said, "There are some trees now. I like trees. Isn't it about evening? It's cooler."

"Michael, let's stop," Joe added. "It looks like a good place to camp."

"Don't you think it's a nice place to camp?" David asked.

"It's early yet; besides, we can't stop until we come to water. Pioneers didn't make a dry camp unless it was absolutely necessary. You're supposed to be such big guys. Never get tired! Hah!"

A car whizzed by, leaving a cloud of dust in their faces.

"We ought to have a big car," Joe scowled. "We could get there in one day."

"We'd have to leave Red 'n' Jake 'n' Nanny 'n' Goldie," Betty objected. "They wouldn't like that."

Another car came along. The people leaned out the window, staring at them.

"They sure look," Joe growled.

"You're crabby," Linda said. "Who cares how much they stare? I suppose we look funny to them. I see no one else traveling with a donkey."

"I wish we could go in a boat down the river or fly an airplane. We wouldn't have to walk then, and nobody would stare." Joe did wish they could stop. His legs were beginning to hurt, his head was hot, and the old road was rough.

"We've done fine so far," Michael encouraged them. "I think the road crosses a river soon. We'll find a camping place for tonight. Then we can start early in the morning when it's cool."

"Good," they all agreed, forgetting their tired legs at the thought of stopping.

Soon Joe spotted a bridge up the road. "Come on, David. Let's run. We'll find a place."

They raced to the bridge, with the dog loping along beside them, then turned off the road into a large grassy area by the river. It was cool under the big maple trees, and the thick green grass felt good to their feet when they took their shoes off.

"We can hide our shoes in these bushes until the rest get here with the cart," Joe suggested.

Stooping over the edge of the river, they dashed water on their faces. "Um, feels good," David mumbled.

"This is a good place to sleep, right here," Joe said. "But, remember, we can't drink this water. Michael says river water has to be boiled. It might have germs."

"Maybe, but Red's sure not afraid of germs. Look at him lap it up."

"Hey, David! See those two big logs nailed together. That looks like a raft. That's the kind kids have when they run away in stories."

The boys went over to inspect the raft. "It's long," David marveled. They rolled their pants up and waded out to the raft. After Joe climbed on, he found a long, smooth board lying in the crack between the logs.

"What's that?" David asked.

"It's to paddle with," Joe replied, as he helped his

brother scramble up beside him. "You put it down deep in the bottom of the river and push. The raft scoots out in the river. Then you paddle."

David helped Joe push out into the middle of the stream. The current wasn't strong, so they had to push and paddle to keep the raft going. They took turns with the board as they talked about traveling on a raft with food and blankets.

After a while David said, "I'm tired. Besides I think the others are at the bridge. We better go back."

"Let's go down to that turn first."

David kept the raft moving, and they soon reached the bend in the river. "Let's go back," he urged.

"All right," Joe agreed as he took the board to push and guide the raft upstream. But he quickly found it was much harder to go upstream than down. He pushed and panted. It seemed like every time he got a little way up stream, he would float back twice as far. "We've got to get this raft back. It belongs to somebody, and I wish we'd never taken it."

Just then the raft swirled around and around. Losing his balance, Joe dropped the board in the water. "Hang on, David! We got to. It's deep here."

The raft straightened out and shot downstream, gaining speed each second. "The water's going faster," David wailed. "I wish we knew how to swim."

"Hang on, David!" Joe cried frantically. "Maybe it'll bump into something and stop."

But the raft didn't bump into anything, and it didn't stop, and the water kept getting swifter. They bounded along, spinning around, being jerked to the right and then to the left. As the raft bounced around one bend, David slipped off the log into the water, grabbing the log just in time to avoid going under.

Joe edged over and took hold of his arm. All at once someone yelled, "Hang on! It'll hit a sandbar down a way. Hang on!"

Then the water changed course and headed the raft to the left. It hit something, bumped, and stopped. The boys went scooting over the slippery raft to the sand.

As they picked themselves up, an old man with long white whiskers and hair came hurrying toward them. "Told you you'd hit sand. Mighty good thing you hung on. You have to know this river."

Joe stared at the old man. His beard waved back and forth when he talked, and he slapped his leg at the end of every sentence.

"Come on, David. Are you OK?" Joe asked.

"I'm all right, but I'm cold."

"I'll build a fire at my place and get you warmed up," the old man announced. "Probably just shock."

The twins followed him because they couldn't think of anything better to do. "Come on, young'uns. Hurry up! You're just like all the kids nowadays, a little on the soft side and slow. Ain't nothin' like the old days."

Trying to keep up with the old man, Joe and David walked faster. Joe didn't like to be called soft.

"Mister, what's you name?" David asked.

The old fellow chuckled, nodding his white head, making his hair and beard wave back and forth. "Well, boys, my folks named me Christopher James Johnson. My friends called me Chris. I reckon you can call me that.

That's what everybody called me when I was trappin'. Those days are gone, and folks just call me that crazy old coot who holes up down the river and don't live civilized."

"They aren't very polite," David said. "Our mother says we shouldn't expect everybody to live the same way. She says everybody has a right to choose."

"You must have a pretty smart mother," Chris said.

David smiled. "She's the best. She's real sick and in a sanitarium. We try to remember everything she taught us. We want her to be proud of us."

"Yes," Joe interrupted. "That's why we have to get the raft back. I don't know why we used it. We don't want anyone to think we stole it. Do you know how we can get it back?"

Chris shook his head and looked back at the boys. "I'll tell you, anybody with a mother like you have can't be too bad. At first I was real put out about that raft. It's mine. I made it up the river and planned on bringing my winter supplies down on it. It took me about an hour to rig it up. Suppose you boys work for me an hour. Then we'll call it square. I can make another raft."

Joe sighed. He felt better already.

"We can do just about anything if you show us how," David told Chris.

"Michael says we're the handymen in the outfit," Joe added.

Chris scratched his head. "Who's Michael?"

"Michael's our big brother," David explained. "He's 12, and he's head of the family while Mom's gone. Linda's next. She's our sister. She's 11, and Betty's 5. We're twins, and we're 7."

"Hm. Quite a family! I'll tell you what. You can pile some wood that I cut yesterday. Then if Cynthia's been up to anything, you can help straighten up."

"Who's Cynthia?" Joe asked.

"Cynthia's my partner. You'll see when we get there. Now let's cut the chewin' and git along."

Chapter 3

As the boys followed Chris along the path, Joe wondered if the other children were looking for them. What had happened to Red? Had he gone back to the cart when they got on the raft? How far was it to Chris's home? He didn't dare ask, afraid Chris would think he was tired and soft. And who was Cynthia?

The boys kept up with Chris all the way to his cabin. David was no longer cold, and their clothes had dried.

"Here's the wood," Chris laughed. "Pile it up close to the cabin. I got to feed the chickens and milk my goats, then we'll go in and feed our faces."

"We have a goat too," David said. "Linda says we won't starve because Nanny gives us her milk and Goldie gives us an egg every day."

Chris raised his eyebrows. "Hm! You boys hurry up."

They worked hard piling the big chunks neatly against the cabin. When they were through, Chris came around the corner. "Say! You young'uns have paid for your ride on my raft. This is a good job. Come on and meet Cynthia. You'll see the liberties a partner takes."

Looking around the crude cabin, they saw a rough wooden table in the middle of the room and a bed made out of more rough lumber nailed to the wall. A few articles of clothing hung on nails by the bed. A shelf nailed to the wall had a mail-order catalog on it. In one corner squatted an old iron stove and more board shelves for dishes, pots, and pans. A wooden box with a tin wash pan on it stood by the door. Another box held a pail of water.

The most interesting thing was a pile of objects in front of the door. A pair of rubber boots, some magazines, a few tin cups, a blanket, and three or four chunks of wood all in one neat pile.

Chris laughed. "That's Cynthia's work. She's trying to dam up the doorway."

Joe's eyes shifted from the pile of things to one of Chris's homemade chairs. It seemed to have only three legs and had toppled over on the floor.

"I don't care if she chewed the leg off that chair. I've been threatening to get rid of all my chairs and sit on chunks of wood," Chris said. "I don't like her damming up the doorway, though. I see she's been trying to make a lodge under my bed. Must be about 25 sticks of kindling there."

The boys stared at one strange thing after the other, then back at Chris. "You sure have a funny partner," David said. "Where is she?"

"She's over there sleeping by the stove, never figuring she's done anything wrong."

They hurried over to the stove and gazed down at a big ball of brown fur with a large flat paddle-like tail. "It's a beaver, David. Remember the one at the fair?" Joe exclaimed.

"That's what it is," David replied. "Will she bite, Chris?"

"No, she won't bite. She's tame as a dog or a cat. But

she has one trouble. She can't get over her beaver habits of building dams and lodges and chewing every piece of wood she gets near. Come on now. Let's put this stuff away."

As soon as everything was in order, the boys went back to Cynthia. They stooped over and petted her.

"Now we'll stir up something to eat," Chris said.

"I don't know if we ought to stay," Joe said. "The others are going to be awfully worried about us."

"I been figuring on that. You young'uns probably couldn't find the way alone. After we eat I'll walk back with you."

"Good," David said. "How'd you tame Cynthia?"

As Chris measured out flour and things for biscuits he explained, "I found her near a pool of water off the river when she was just a little baby. There was a fox sneakin' around, trying to get her. He left when he saw me. I brought her home, and she's been with me ever since. Last winter she wanted to fix up everything."

"What did she do?" Joe asked.

"It was a windy winter. Cold wind came through the cracks between the logs in the cabin. It didn't bother me much, but Cynthia didn't like it. She'd work hours filling those cracks. When I'd miss my dish towel and almost anything else, I'd know where to look. Cynthia'd have 'em poked in between the logs."

The boys laughed and petted the beaver some more until she woke up. She seemed to like their attention and rubbed against their legs, dragging her big flat tail on the floor.

Joe watched Chris break eggs in a bowl: one, two,

three, four, five, six, seven, eight, nine. He lost count. "I never saw so many eggs cracked at once! Never!" Joe exclaimed.

"I have lots of eggs, and I figure you boys are hungry."

The boys set the table and brought a box and two large chunks of wood to sit on.

"It's a nice dinner. I wish the others could have some," David said

"Do you think they'd like bachelor stew?" Chris asked as he put huge helpings of thick savory soup and vegetables on their plates.

"Oh, they'd think it was just great," David replied. Joe agreed with him.

The boys ate piles of golden scrambled eggs, one after another of Chris's light flaky biscuits, and several helpings of bachelor stew.

"I'm sure full," David said, just as they heard a knock on the door and a couple of loud barks.

"There's Red. He's found us! Red's found us!" Joe yelled in excitement. Joe and David rushed with Chris to the door. There stood Michael and Red.

While the twins explained what had happened, Chris started breaking eggs into a bowl again.

Michael listened to the boys' story. "You boys had us worried when Red showed up alone." He frowned. "You had no business running off that way. We should stay together. I've been looking all over for you. If it hadn't been for Red's help, I wouldn't have found you. Whose raft did you take?"

"The raft belongs to Chris," Joe answered. "We piled wood for him to pay for the ride. We're sorry."

Soon Chris had Michael at the table devouring food. "Michael can't be angry with good food to eat, not when he's so hungry," Joe thought to himself.

"Don't you worry, Michael," Chris said. "The boys have caused a little trouble, but they've paid for what they did. I'm going to walk home with you. Everything'll be fine."

Just then they heard a gnawing sound. Chris reached down and pulled Cynthia out from under the table. "Now listen here, young lady. You leave these table legs alone. We don't want the dinner on the floor."

Michael laughed. "That's a funny pet. Betty sure would like to play with her. If she traveled with us, she'd chew holes in the floor of the cart and fall out."

Chris passed Michael more food and leaned back in his chair. "There ain't nothing safe around here with that partner of mine. This spring, old Jonas Campbell came down here in a rowboat. He was takin' census. Knew I was here and nobody else. I don't know why he had to come, but he did. Well, he hobbled up the trail to my place, then came in and snooped around. I had him eat dinner with me. We were getting along fine, him telling me how crazy I was to live here all alone, way off from nowhere, and me trying awful hard not to say anything mean to him. Only thing, he didn't know about my partner and her hankerin' for chewin' wood. If he had, he'd been more careful, him with a wooden leg. He got his own sawed off when he had blood poison one time. Anyway, Cynthia got herself under the table and started chewin' away on Jonas' wooden leg. Old Jonas stood up. He was longer on one side and like to fell down."

"What did he do then?" David asked.

"Aw, we nailed an extension onto what was left of his wooden leg. He got home all right—he didn't mind. Fact was, he was plannin' on gettin' some kind of a new-fangled leg at the store. All he needed was a little help decidin' when."

The boys laughed and petted Cynthia some more.

"We have to get started as soon as we clean up the dishes," Michael said. "Linda and Betty will be worried, and besides they might get scairt all alone. You know girls. It's getting dark."

"I've been piecin' things together and thinkin' over everything you young'uns been tellin' me, and I ain't got it figured out yet. Are you runnin' away from somebody, or what? Who was supposed to be stayin' with you? Is somebody lookin' after you?"

"Oh, none of those things. We're on our way to Grandma's," Michael answered.

"Is it far?" Chris asked.

"This morning when we started it was 85 miles," David explained. "Michael says we have to go 10 miles a day and some extra."

"With a goat and a chicken!" Chris exclaimed.

"We have a donkey too. His name is Jake, and he's pulling the cart."

Michael and Joe looked at each other. Would Chris try to stop them? Squaring his shoulders, Michael stood up from the table. "Well, beings you know everything else, you might as well know we had tickets to go on the train, but Nanny Goat grabbed the tickets from Betty and ate them. You know how goats eat everything. So

31

we have to walk. We couldn't worry our mother about it because she's very sick in a sanitarium. And we couldn't ask Grandma to buy tickets. Please don't tell anyone. They might write to our mother. She would be upset and get worse."

"Don't you worry about me, boy," Chris laughed. "I wouldn't tell anybody for the world. I guess all the kids ain't gone soft after all. The spirit of the West ain't dead yet. No, we won't tell anybody. They'd meddle. You'll get along all right. Nothin' for anybody to worry about."

All three boys glanced at each other and sighed in relief.

As he talked and laughed, Chris dropped one egg after another into a kettle of boiling water on the stove. Then he put the rest of the stew in a quart jar. After they finished the dishes, he placed the now hard-boiled eggs and the jar of stew in a bag and handed it to Michael. "Oh, boy, all of us will have some nice dinner after all!" David shouted.

Chris gave Red a big bowl of scraps and petted him. "First dog I ever saw who didn't fight Cynthia."

Soon the boys and Chris started off through the trees toward the bridge. It was dark, but the moon shone bright and gave them light to see by.

When they spotted the girls, the twins yelled, "Linda! Betty! Here we are!"

The two sisters came running to meet them. Everyone was so excited to see each other that no one could understand anything anyone else said. Finally they managed to get the whole story out from the ride on the raft to Cynthia.

"You are a nice man, Chris, to take care of my twins," Betty said, taking hold of his old hand. "And thank you for the good food. It would take Goldie forever to lay that many eggs. Jesus will be kind to you for helping us."

The old man looked thoughtful. "You're good kids."

The children thanked him again before he started home. He shook hands with them and smiled. "If you ever come by again, drop by and see me, but not on a raft. Now I gotta get back to my partner before she eats the house down."

Linda and Betty ate the stew while they talked over what had happened that day.

When the girls finished eating, Michael said, "The twins and I will make a bed under this big tree, by the cart. Linda, you and Betty make yours in the cart. I think it's long enough if you don't stretch out too much. I have one end of the cart resting on a stump so it won't tip over."

Michael and the twins broke off little bushes growing near the tree and piled them together for beds. Then each one of the boys rolled up in a blanket on their new "mattresses."

Linda and Betty took all the things out of the cart. Then they shook the clothes from the laundry bag and smoothed them out in the bottom of the cart to make their bed softer. After Linda spread her blanket out on the clothes, they used Betty's blanket for a cover.

Everyone turned and tossed in their unfamiliar beds several times until Michael yelled, "From now on don't anybody go off like that again. We're supposed to stay together, understand?"

"We won't," they all answered.

In a short time David whispered, "It's dark, and the trees look black. It's lonesome here."

"It sure is," Joe agreed. "I never thought about night."

"Now don't start anything like being afraid of the dark, because we'll sleep out about six more times," Michael ordered. "There isn't any sense to it anyway. Red's here to protect us. He'd chew anything to pieces if it bothered us."

"I'm going to cover my head and pretend I'm home," Betty said, her voice trembling. "I'll hang on to Linda's hand too. Then it'll seem like always."

"We'll say our verses like Mother told us to," Linda added. "Then we'll feel better and go to sleep. Who remembers the one about the angel encamping?"

"I know that. It was our memory verse last Sabbath. 'The angel of the Lord encampeth round about them that fear him, and delivereth them' (Psalm 34:7)," Joe quoted.

"Fine, Joe. That means an angel will guard us," Linda reassured them.

"I'm glad we have angel guards," Betty said.

"Nobody could get by angel guards," Joe declared loudly.

Betty was the first one asleep.

Chapter Four

By morning the children had forgotten about being frightened and lonely. After a breakfast of Nanny's milk and the hard-boiled eggs Chris gave them, they tended to the business of covering as much distance as possible until eleven o'clock. Then they came to a clump of small pine trees huddled with a huge maple. Under the trees stood two dilapidated-looking outside rest rooms. Oil cans and other clutter led to an old gas pump in front of a small weather-beaten store.

Michael halted Jake near the rest rooms, and the children took turns going in. Each had a drink from a hose near the gas pump. Michael put water in the white pail and gave Jake a drink, then Nanny and Red.

A man in dirty coveralls came around the side of the building and demanded, "What are you kids hangin' around here for?"

"Just getting a drink," Michael answered, noticing out of the corner of his eye that Joe and David were going into the store. Why hadn't he told them to stay outside?

"Well, take that stinkin' mule and your goat away from here. Where's you folks, anyway? Funny mess, if you ask me. Hurry up!"

Michael hurried. He took Jake and Nanny across

the road and told a very quiet Linda and Betty to stay there while he went after the boys.

Michael opened the door to call the twins, and Red slipped ahead of him, bounded up on first David, then Joe, pressing his front feet on their chests, licking their faces and wagging his tail as if he hadn't seen them for weeks.

"Get that dog out of here! Get that dog out of here!" a woman screeched from behind the counter. Michael noticed her coveralls were slightly cleaner than the man's.

The noise excited Red. He raced back and forth between Michael and the twins, his tail brushing against dusty cans and a few loaves of bread.

"I'll get the dog catcher," the woman screamed.

While Michael called Red, Joe and David tried to grab him, but the dog was having a good time. Excitedly he ran behind the counter, swooshing everything with his tail. A clatter echoed throughout the store as a thin glass pitcher fell to the floor shattering into many pieces.

"Look," screeched the woman. "That was the prize. That was the prize on the punchboard. You pay, or I'm calling the dog catcher."

Grabbing the animal by the collar, Michael led him out the door, with the boys and the woman following.

"Take Red to the cart," he ordered Joe. "Keep him there."

The woman was still yelling, "Pay! Pay!" Michael took a dollar bill from his pocket and handed it to the woman.

Although she exclaimed, "It's not enough," she calmed down and added, "but just get out of here."

Quietly and gently the children urged Jake down the road. Even Betty realized that all their money was now gone. They traveled without stopping until evening when

David pointed out a small clump of trees to camp under.

The following morning Linda had Michael build a fire to cook the beans on. They put a large rock on each side of the fire so the red kettle would set straight. The beans were soon boiling, but they ate them before they were good like Mother cooked, for Michael said they didn't have time to wait any longer. It was a small package of beans; so they finished them all for breakfast.

At lunch time they built another fire to cook the macaroni and make a tiny pudding out of Goldie's little egg. Afterward Linda handed out the last of the apples and said, "We have salt and a little sugar and flour in the grocery box. That's all."

"You're kidding," Michael groaned. "What happened to the potatoes?"

"That's what I'd like to know," she replied. "They were in the cart. They must have bounced out somewhere. Anyway, they're gone."

"Did you look good?" he persisted.

"I looked and I searched. We had only five, and that was enough for supper."

"Well, let's get started."

Red gulped down his share of macaroni and gave a couple of happy yips as they loaded the now very light grocery box back into the cart. He barked some more as they returned with the empty red kettle and the white pail.

Michael glared at the dog. "This is your fault. If you hadn't run into the store and broken that pitcher . . . Joe, you and David had no business in there either. Of course Red would follow," he sighed. "The truth is, I shouldn't blame Red."

In the afternoon they stopped to investigate a creek for fish and crawdads. "All I see are little tiny ones," David complained.

"Tiny ones are better than nothing—if you eat fish," Linda commented. "Probably all we'll have for supper is a sip of milk, but I'm not eating fish. They might be infected or something. Mother would be very sorry if we started eating meat."

"How many pop bottles do we have?" Michael asked suddenly.

Joe ran to the cart and counted the bottles they had picked up along the road. "Fourteen," he yelled out. "That's enough for a loaf of bread."

"There's a store up the road. Linda, you and David go after the bread. Joe and I'll stay here with Betty and keep Red. We don't want any more funny business," Michael suggested.

"All right," Linda agreed. "It's probably a mile. We'll have to travel the same way again when we go on."

"Oh no, we don't! We turn to the right about halfway to the store. You should have watched when we went with the Smith's to the beach," Michael grumbled. "Girls always make things sound worse than they are. It isn't a mile either."

"OK, Michael, have fun playing in the creek. Let's go, David."

They put the bottles in an onion bag from the grocery box and started out.

As they walked, the afternoon sun grew hotter. "David, my head aches something awful," the girl complained. "You're a big boy, 7 years old. Take the bottles and go to the store. I'll sit here in the grass and wait for you."

David felt important that Linda had asked him to go alone. He would do anything for Linda because she helped all of them. Sometimes she was almost like Mom instead of just a sister. Besides, it was his fault they had gone into the store, where Red broke the pitcher. It had been his idea to go in and look around.

Standing tall and swinging the sack of bottles, he replied, "You stay here and rest. I'll hurry."

About halfway to the store David stopped to look at a big cornfield. Not much corn remained, for a machine was mowing it down. "It looks like it's eating the field," he thought to himself. "Mean old pig eating all that good corn. I wish we had some of it."

Walking to the edge of the field, he watched how the machine worked. A tractor pulled the machine as it cut the stalks close to the ground. The cornstalks and leaves spewed to the ground out of a big spout, but the ears of corn dropped onto a truck bed. The machine didn't throw all the corn on the truck. Sometimes an ear fell to the ground with the cornstalks and leaves.

The tractor and machine rounded the corner of the field and stopped in front of him. The man in the truck yelled to the tractor driver, "I'll take the load up."

"Fine," the other man answered, then turned the motor off and started checking something on the tractor.

Glancing up, the truck driver saw David. "Do you like to watch?"

"Yes," David replied. "Are you going to pick up the corn that landed on the ground instead of on the truck?"

"There isn't much. We probably won't bother. Couldn't be more than a gunnysack full."

Excited, David jumped the ditch and approached the man. "There's enough corn scattered around here for all my brothers and sisters. Would you take these pop bottles for some of the corn? I was supposed to trade them for a loaf of bread, but I think corn would be better."

The man looked down at the pop bottles David carried in the onion sack. Pushing his hat back, he scratched behind his ear. "Well, so you want to trade. Sounds good to me, only I have no use for pop bottles."

David's heart did three quick thuds. He'd thought for sure the man would trade.

"What's your name?"

"My name's David. I'm a twin. Joe's my twin brother. He's back at the creek with Michael. Michael's my oldest brother."

"David, to tell the truth, I'd like to have you pick up that scattered corn. You take your bottles up to the store and get your bread. When you return, pick up all the corn you can find. Here's a gunnysack to put it in."

He pulled a sack off the floor of the tractor and handed it to David. "How are you going to get the corn home?" he asked. "A sack of corn is pretty heavy."

"I'll get Jake. Jake's our donkey. We have a cart too. We'll put the corn in the cart."

"How far do you live from here, David?" the man continued in a friendly way.

David's heart skipped again. Was the man going to cause trouble? Would he call the sanitarium and make their mother worse? Why hadn't he left the corn alone and just gone on his way? His brothers and sisters could go without any supper.

After a long pause David managed to answer, "We're going to live with our grandma soon. She has a farm, too. Mother says everything will be all right then."

The man smiled. "David, I'm sure everything's going to turn out fine for you. I won't be here when you come back from the store, but you go ahead and get the corn anyway. This field goes right by the store. Do you want to ride the rest of the way with me?"

"Oh, boy!" David cried, forgetting all about being afraid as the farmer helped him up on the big tractor.

Jerked into gear, it bumped along. David had never ridden on one before. Now he would have something to tell the others!

When they reached the store he said, "I'm not sure my mom'd want me to take the corn without paying for it. She says it's not fair to take things for nothing. I could get the money for the bottles and give it to you."

The man shook his head. "I'm glad to have you pick up the corn, David. If you didn't, it would be wasted, or I'd be out there picking it up myself when I ought to be doing something else. A farm's a busy place, you know. I'm glad you're going to take care of that corn. You don't owe me a thing."

"OK. I'll tell the others I helped you keep busy at important things by picking up the corn."

They laughed together, and David went into the store for his loaf of bread. Then he trudged back to the gunnysack and started hunting for stray ears of corn the machine had left in the field.

He was happy about the corn, but the sun was still hot and his long hair hung down over his eyes. He

41

stooped over, running his hand through the foliage to find any dropped ears. Whenever he found one, he dropped it into the sack.

Finally he stood up, rubbing his back. It ached from bending over. "Hurts like bee stings," he muttered.

Pushing his hair away from his face again, he blew his breath up toward his nose. It didn't cool his face, though. With a sigh he began to hunt for some more corn. When the sack was half full he took it over by the fence post where he had left the bread. Then back across the field he searched. He tried to think of the empty grocery box and how Linda would fill the red kettle with roasting ears for supper, of how happy everybody would be with them.

His arms full, he staggered to the gunny sack, then back to the field again. Back and forth until the sack stood straight and tall against the fence post.

It was full. He could have had the other children help, but he wanted to surprise them. Now all he had to do was get Jake. Eager to tell what he had, he ran until he came to the tall grass where he had left Linda. She was lying asleep in the grass, her legs hanging down in a dry ditch.

"Wake up!" he called.

Linda opened her eyes and sat up. "David Larkin! I've waited and waited. What have you been up to? Where's the bread?"

"It's by the cornfield."

She frowned. "What cornfield? Did you leave our bread in a cornfield? What's the matter with you? Go get it right away."

"Linda! Linda! I got a whole sack of corn ears, honest." Then he explained about the whole things.

"Oh, David! Isn't that perfectly wonderful? Jesus is taking care of us. Jesus won't let us down."

David couldn't feel the bee stings in his back as he and Linda ran to the others. Her head didn't seem to hurt anymore either.

"You sure took your time," Michael greeted them. "And where's the bread?"

"Come on, bring Jake," David said. "I've got a whole sack of corn ears!"

"Corn ears!" everyone exclaimed.

David told the whole story again.

"Oh, boy!" Joe cried. "Let's go!"

Jake looked annoyed at the children for starting out again, and Nanny jerked from Linda as if to say, "This is a good place to stay. What's the idea?"

When they reached the fence post where the sack of corn stood, the children peered into the sack and felt the big ears of corn. Betty pulled the silk from one of the ears. "Lovely corn tassels and lovely corn."

"David's a good twin," Joe said. "Isn't he, Michael? This takes the place of the dollar. Doesn't it?"

"He's a good brother," the oldest boy answered. "He's got our supper for us. Let's forget the dollar. Accidents happen."

David felt good inside because everyone was happy, and they were going to forget about the pitcher Red broke.

"Now," Linda said, "everybody can have a slice of bread, because we're hungry and can't eat until we find a place to cook the corn unless we go back to the creek."

"Fine idea, Linda," Michael agreed. "Of course we won't go back. We've got to keep moving on." He turned to David. "You sure fixed us up with corn. Let's get it into the cart and nobody rides. This is load enough for Jake when it's hot."

"But after supper we can ride again, because we'll eat so many ears it won't be heavy for Jake," Betty said.

The children laughed, and each took a slice of bread. It was quite cool before they found a place to stop.

"We have to have trees," Michael said, "so curious people can't see we're alone."

"And we need grass for Nanny and Jake," Joe added.

"And grasshoppers for Goldie," Betty piped up.

"And a big fire for David's corn," Linda said.

Their camp had everything but water. Michael sent Joe to a farmhouse with the white pail for water, warning him not to say much, because if he didn't talk he wouldn't give away much.

Linda brought the red kettle. She and David pulled the husks off the corn so it would be ready for cooking.

By the time Joe returned and they had the fire built and the goat milked, the children were so hungry they could hardly wait for the corn. "This is once we'll get all the roasting ears we want," Linda said as she passed them around.

The children didn't talk while they ate. The only sound was that of their teeth zooming up and down the roasting ears. David didn't ask if they liked the corn. All he had to do was look at the growing pile of corncobs and listen to the water in the red kettle bubbling as Linda boiled more.

When they had eaten all they could hold, she announced, "All David has to do is go to sleep, because he earned our supper." The rest of the children helped put things away as neatly as possible without water to wash dishes. Then because they were so tired and so full, they curled up in their blankets for the night.

"Is anyone scared?" David whispered. "It's real dark, and we're all alone."

"Come on, David! You know better than that," Michael answered. "This is our third night out. Nothing has happened yet. I thought everyone was over that. Remember the angel guards around us. They make us safe. If you really want to worry, here's something to think about. How are five of us—and a donkey, a goat, a hen, a dog, and a cart—going to get through a big town like Cheqasa tomorrow? There will be policemen everywhere, and I don't know how many curious people."

"We'll have to get through someway," Linda replied. "We want Mom to get better."

"We'll pray about that too," Betty said.

"Of course we will," Linda agreed.

Each one prayed for the angel guards to stay by them and for help the next day.

Chapter Five

Linda prepared the rest of the roasting ears for breakfast the next morning, and each child had a cup of Nanny's milk. "You're a good goat, Nanny, even if you did eat our tickets," she commented as she drank the milk. David cut corn off the cob for Red, who gulped the kernels down greedily.

After breakfast they hurried around getting ready to travel. Linda put the leftover corn into their old bread wrapper for lunch. The boys shook all the blankets and folded them neatly. The dog ran from first one to the other, barking joyfully as if to say, "This is fun. Come on. Hurry. Let's get going!"

"I read about a pioneer family who used dry ashes to get their pots and pans clean after they cooked on a campfire," Linda said finally. "I'm going to try it, even if you are in a hurry, Red. This black smoke on the kettle will get everything dirty."

She rubbed ashes on the outside of the red kettle and scrubbed hard. When Joe brought the water, she rinsed the kettle off several times. Soon she had it shining like new. "It works!" she exclaimed.

Michael hitched the donkey to the cart, and Joe tied the goat to the back. Betty perched Goldie on Jake's back, and they started on their way.

They were in good spirits, but by afternoon the little group began poking. The sun shone its hardest, and Michael could feel his clothes beginning to stick to his body. The rocks on the road seemed to get harder and sharper until he could feel them through the soles of his shoes.

Michael rubbed his face with the sleeve of his shirt and worried to himself. "I'm the oldest and most responsible for what happens to us. The groceries are gone, and we don't have any money. David's shoes are worn through, and his feet are sore. At least he's doing better since he and Joe take turns wearing Joe's shoes. Nanny isn't giving as much milk as she did at home. Jake's limping on one foot. It's just a few miles to Cheqasa. How are we going to get through a big town like that? We'll attract attention with a lame donkey. Goldie'll probably start cackling on Main Street, and Betty'll show her to the mayor or somebody else. I should have thought things out before we started on this trip. And I wonder if Uncle Cecil has discovered anything about us yet?

"Better let Jake rest his leg," he said out loud to the others. "No one should ride him. Then maybe he'll get over limping." He pulled on the little donkey's reins, and it sighed with relief at a chance to stop.

Betty took the little hen off Jake's back. "Goldie isn't too heavy for Jake, but she's hungry. She wants bugs and grasshoppers." The chicken stretched and flapped her wings in the dry grass by the road.

"I guess that's what she wants," Michael agreed, wishing he could find food as easily as Goldie. The cold ears of corn hadn't filled them.

"Michael," Linda yelled. "Stop the boys! Stop them right now!"

He glanced back over his shoulder, then handed Jake's reins to her and ran toward the twins.

"These are my shoes anyway. I'm tired of wearing your old worn-out ones. You wear mine more than I do. Now give 'em to me," he heard Joe saying as the two boys rolled on the ground, each one trying to get the shoes that had fallen from David's hands.

As he separated the boys, he thought, "David's crying. There must be something the matter. He never cries." He pulled David over toward him, and they sat down. Joe squatted beside them. "Now what's the matter?" Michael asked. "It better be good, too, or I'm going to paddle the pair of you. I mean it."

They looked at him in surprise. "David wants my shoes all the time," Joe explained. "I think I ought to wear them the most because they're mine. I trade part of the time, but his are all worn out."

"I don't want them all the time. Besides, I just wanted one," David objected.

"Why one?" Michael asked David.

"Because one foot's too fat. I can't get his shoe on the fat one. It hurts too," David said, holding his foot up.

As Michael inspected the foot, he gasped. David's foot was terribly swollen and bright red.

"Are there any red streaks up his leg?" Linda asked over his shoulder. "If there are, he's got blood poison."

Carefully Michael pulled the pant leg up. "No streaks of red, but it looks bad."

"Ouch," David cried as Michael touched his ankle

close to a small cut. "That's where I jagged it on a rock."

"It has dirt in the cut," Linda observed. "That's why it's so sore."

"Do you suppose he needs a doctor?" Michael asked her.

"If he does, how are we going to pay for one? Besides, a doctor would ask questions."

"That's right," Michael muttered.

"Mom told me when she was little her brother had an infection in his hand. They soaked it in real hot water. And they put a lot of salt in the water too."

"Do we have any salt?" Michael asked quickly.

"That's one thing we have a whole box of. We could build a fire and heat water, if we could find a place."

"We'll try it. If it doesn't work by evening, we'll have to find a doctor, no matter what!"

"Michael, are you going to soak Jake's foot too?" Betty asked.

"I think a good rest and green grass will fix Jake up."

"David can have the shoes," Joe offered. "I didn't know his foot was sore."

"Of course you didn't," Linda comforted him.

"Come on, everybody," Michael announced. "We've got to find a camp. You know the pioneers stopped when their animals got tired and someone was sick." He helped David into the cart, then patted the donkey on the back. "Come on, Jake. You can walk a little farther, even with David. We'll have to get off the road if we don't want someone watching us."

"There's a railroad," Linda observed. "Looks like an old road by it. Up a ways are some trees."

"We have to be where there's water," Michael

replied. "It looks like there might be a creek there. I see some willows. Willows grow near water."

The children stayed close together as they turned down the old road that was nothing but two tracks. Grass and bushes grew on both sides of it and down the middle.

Jake limped as he pulled the creaking cart, but Michael talked to him to keep him going. The others trailed behind the cart, each feeling a little homesick and alone.

But as they entered a grove of trees Jake perked up and made a straight line to the little creek. He took a long drink and sighed. The goat happily nibbled first at the leaves hanging down from a tree, then at grass. Betty tied Goldie to a small bush. The little hen scratched in the dirt and snapped her beak at insects.

"Somebody's camped here before," Michael stated. "Here's big rocks in a circle with a tin thing over the top. That's a good stove." The children gathered around.

"You and Joe find wood right away," Linda told Michael. "Start a fire. I'll unhitch Jake and stake him out so he can eat and get rested up."

Michael and Joe soon had a fire going. They put the white pail and the red kettle full of water on the tin to heat. Later Joe yelled from behind a clump of bushes, "Look what I found." Glancing around to see him dragging an old bench, Michael went over to help him, and soon they had it by the cart. Linda put a blanket on the bench, and Michael helped David onto the seat they had fixed.

"I guess the pail's big enough," Linda remarked as Michael set it steaming on the ground by David's feet.

"Now, David, you'll have to get used to it gradually,"

Michael warned as he held the swollen foot close to the steam from the pail.

"I'm not putting my foot in there," David wailed as he squirmed. "It's hot. You want to boil me because there's only one pair of shoes."

Michael rubbed his hand through his hair, thinking, *I never thought about anybody getting sick or hurt. We're always healthy. None of us have ever had to stay home from school. I wish we were home and Mother was there to direct us. There's sure a lot to being the oldest and the one to have to decide about things. It's up to Linda and me to decide everything.*

Aloud he said, "Don't act this way, David. This will make your foot the right size so you can wear both of Joe's shoes."

"Yes," said Joe. "I'm tired of shoes anyway. I won't ever wear shoes again."

"David!" Linda added. "You have to do it. You wouldn't want us to take you to the doctor. He'd ask a lot of questions. Then he'd call Mom and Grandma. They'd know what we're up to. The money wouldn't be saved at all. And Uncle Cecil would find us. We've come a long way, David. We can make it the rest of the way too. If Mom found out about what we've done, she'd worry and get worse. You don't want that to happen."

With all the children encouraging him, slowly and gradually David slipped his foot into the water. He left it in a few seconds, then pulled it out. He did it over and over.

"And, David," Betty promised, "the next time Goldie lays an egg, you can have it because you got a hurted foot." Her brother smiled bravely and continued soaking his foot, even when they poured in more hot water from the red kettle.

"Come on, Joe," Michael said, "we've got to get a big pile of wood." The boys found dead limbs, and Michael cut them up with the little hatchet. They carried the chunks over by the fire. When they had a large pile, they sat down to rest.

"Linda, can you keep David's foot soaking the rest of the day?" Michael asked.

"I think so. Why?"

"I saw some farms up the road from where we turned in. Maybe I could get a job for the rest of the day. We can't go on with David anyway."

She gazed at him, smiling. "Oh, Michael, do you suppose you could? There isn't a thing in the grocery box except salt and about half a cup of flour. We ate all the corn for lunch. You're only 12. They might ask a lot of questions."

"I'll have to take a chance. Joe, you and Betty help Linda. Don't anybody run off. Red, don't let anything bother them," he ordered as he started back the way they had come.

"Michael Larkin, you come right back here," Linda yelled. "Your other shirt's clean. Besides, you can wash up. Nobody lets dirty kids around."

His face turned red, but he went to the creek and scrubbed his face and hands. *Linda's always bossing about soap and water,* he thought. *Funny thing, she's usually right.*

Changing his shirt, he started out again with Linda's warning to be careful not to tell anybody anything important. Michael thought about his brother as he walked, and he prayed, "Jesus, please help David be OK when I get back. Help me to earn some money. If I did wrong in bringing the kids this way to Grandma's forgive me and protect us from Uncle Cecil."

He sighed as he came out on the road. "It's a long way, and I'm hungry. My stomach feels empty. It doesn't seem like I can walk much farther."

As he trudged along he watched his feet. That's when he saw a round, yellow ball. He stopped to pick it up. Betty would like it to play with but it wasn't a ball— it was a rutabaga. Cool and firm, it had probably fallen off a truckload of them, Michael figured as he sat down and took his pocketknife and peeled it. It tasted good. He was beginning to feel better already. Jesus *was* taking care of him.

"Thank You, God," he whispered.

Starting on, he spotted another rutabaga and another and another, then still more. Hurriedly he picked them up, almost laughing with joy. He was sure no one wanted them. The truck driver wouldn't bother to stop if he knew they had fallen off. How many did he have? He counted them—five, and then he found another one—that made six. If it weren't so far, he'd take them back to camp. At last he decided to hide them behind a big rock in the grass. He'd get them on his way back. Michael covered the rutabagas with grass and brush so they wouldn't get hot, and continued on down the road.

He stopped at the first farm and went around back of the house where a man was doing some repair work on a tractor.

"Hello," Michael called.

Tall and with a red face from being out in the sun, the man scowled at Michael and snapped, "What do you want?"

Embarrassed, Michael couldn't think of anything to say. Finally he sputtered, "I thought you might need some help."

"Well, I don't, and I don't want kids hanging around here picking up stuff either."

Michael hurried away. The only things he'd picked up that didn't belong to him were the rutabagas. He was sure they'd have lain there in the road and spoiled if he hadn't gotten them.

At the next place he paused just inside the yard. Maybe no one wanted a boy around. Maybe everybody thought they were all thieves. Probably they didn't need any help here. It didn't seem to be much of a farm. All it had was a vegetable garden at the side of the house and beautiful flowers all over. He might as well go on.

Just then a little old woman stepped out the doorway of the house. "Well, what do I have here? Company! I didn't know you were here."

She was friendly and had such a happy smile. Forgetting all about the other place, he said, "I want to earn some money. I thought you might need a boy around today."

"Oh, I suppose you want money for the celebration tomorrow. Let's see now. Dad's gone to Cheqasa. He's on the grown-ups' parade committee, but I'll think of something. Come on in."

The room was clean and shiny, with a soft rug. He was glad Linda had told him to put on a clean shirt.

"I've been going to wash the woodwork here in the kitchen for several days. Tell you what, I'll give you the job. I have a few other things I don't have time for because I'm baking. Our ladies' club will have a food booth tomorrow."

Michael watched the woman as she talked. She got cleanser, rags, and a pan of water and showed him how to do everything. Then he started to work.

"My name is Mrs. Randall. Everybody around here calls me Ma; you may too. What's you name?"

"I'm Michael Larkin."

"Where do you live, Michael? There are so many new people around I can't keep up with them."

"I don't live here. We're just stopping over for today."

"Is your family traveling far?"

"Not very far. We're going to Petersburg." He added under his breath. "Of course it's a long way if you're walking."

"Petersburg, that's only about 40 miles. You're going to the celebration, then. You ought to get in the parade."

"What kind of a parade is it?" he asked to be courteous, as it seemed she was extremely interested in it.

"There will be two parades. They're both supposed to be pioneer parades. The ones entering who come nearest to fitting pioneer life will get a prize. The young ones' parade is at ten-thirty. Dad wants the parades to start at this end of Cheqasa and go on through town to the other side and end at the fairgrounds. They can give the prizes there. I suppose it'll be that way, too, if I know Dad, and I ought to. I've been married to him 50 years this fall," she explained as she rolled out cookie dough.

"Then there's the adult parade. It's in the afternoon.

We want the kids to be first so they can have fun watching the other parade."

Michael worked away, thinking about the celebration and the parade and sniffing the good smells from her oven.

When he finished with the woodwork, she said, "You're fast and clean too. I think you deserve some refreshments. Let's sit down and have cookies and milk."

He certainly enjoyed the cookies and wished the others could have some. "Can anybody be in the parade?" he asked.

"Of course."

"I mean, even if they don't live in Cheqasa?"

"Oh, yes, anybody. Lots of folks come here from other places."

Michael polished silver and did a special job on pots and pans. He gathered vegetables from the garden, carried canned fruit downstairs and placed it on shelves in the basement, and did everything she asked him to, with a smile.

About five o'clock she said, "Michael, I don't believe there's anything more to do. I'm real pleased. I have all my baking finished. Here's your money. I think this is about right."

She handed him two silver dollars. Michael took the money. *Oh, boy, now if David is better,* he thought to himself, *we can go on tomorrow.*

"Where is your family staying?" she asked.

He hesitated. "We're camping by a little creek up the road." That certainly was all right to say. The other children were his family.

"How nice to be camping. That must be lots of fun, but you can't bake much. I'll send some things with you." Michael watched her put a big loaf of fresh bread and some cookies and rolls in a paper bag.

"This is great. Tonight we'll have a feast. Goodbye, Ma. It was fun working for you."

Mrs. Randall waved at him from the door as he left. She called, "Come and see me anytime you're here, Michael. You're good company."

He hurried up the road, found the rutabagas, stuffed them inside the front of his shirt, and continued on his way.

What a day! He had many things to tell the others and surprises to give them. And he thought he had a whale of an idea, too, an idea that might work, with God's help.

Chapter Six

When Michael reached camp, the children gathered around him, bursting with questions. "First, how's David?" he asked.

"I'm OK," the boy yelled from under a tree where he sat. "Linda boiled me a long time. My foot's not very fat now."

"I think he'll be all right tomorrow morning," she commented.

"What's in the packages?" Joe asked. "Do you have something to eat?"

"And what makes your shirt so fat?" Betty added.

Michael took the rutabagas out of his shirt, and they sat down under the tree to hear about his adventures. He gave each one a big cookie while they listened.

"Yum, yum," Betty murmured. "We'll have a real supper tonight. Linda's going to make a pudding out of Goldie's egg. David wouldn't eat it because we couldn't all have one. So she's going to put flour and milk with it and our teeny bit of sugar. Aren't we having a wonderful time?"

"Yes, we are," Michael agreed.

"I washed all the extra clothes and everybody's hair. We took baths in the creek, all except David," Linda told him. "It was cold, but we have to be clean. Here's the soap, Michael. It's your turn."

He frowned to himself. "This again! Oh, well, better do it." Shortly he came back from the creek, shivering but smiling. The smell of rutabagas cooking filled the air.

They sat down under the tree to eat. Linda piled food on their plates. They had the fresh bread Mrs. Randall had sent and milk to drink. For dessert they had another big fat cookie with Linda's pudding.

"This sure is a good supper you brought," David grinned.

"I didn't bring it all. Nanny gave us milk. Somebody dropped the rutabagas along the road. Besides, where would we be if Linda hadn't cooked it?"

"Yes, and Goldie gave an egg for the pudding," Betty added.

Michael laughed. "No, we won't forget Goldie."

"Let's have a prayer meeting, a 'thank-you' prayer meeting," Linda suggested. They were used to having thank-you prayer meetings at home. Mom had them after every emergency.

Betty choose the first song, "Jesus Loves Me." Joe selected "Dare to Be a Daniel." David wanted to sing "Jesus Loves the Little Children." Linda's favorite was "He's the Lily of the Valley."

After the singing, Michael prayed, "Thank You, Jesus, for making David well again. Thank You again for the food, and Jesus, please help us get through Cheqasa tomorrow. In Jesus' name. Amen."

The dog whined, pushing Michael's arm with his paw. "Red, old boy, we saved some for you. Here's rutabaga with milk." Red lapped his small portion up and licked Michael's hands as if to say, "Thank you."

Michael turned to the children. "I've got an idea about Cheqasa."

"You always think of something, Michael. It usually ends up in walking more, though," Linda complained.

"This is where you're fooled. You won't have to do anything. Only walk right through town. I mean right down Main Street," he beamed.

"Isn't that silly? We don't want a lot of people asking questions," Linda replied in puzzlement.

The children gazed wide-eyed at Michael, waiting for him to explain.

"Remember, I told you about the celebration. There's going to be a kids' parade in the morning. It starts at this end of town and ends at the fairgrounds, which is right by the highway. The old road we travel on is close. It's a pioneer parade."

"I know, I know!" David laughed. "We're just like pioneers."

Betty ran over to Goldie, who was pecking at insects in the grass. "Goldie, do you hear that? We're going to be in a parade."

"It's funny," Linda laughed. "No one will suspect we're just traveling through. Michael, you're real smart."

Michael grinned, feeling warm and happy inside. It made him feel good when Linda thought he did the right thing. If she just didn't harp on washing and being neat all the time.

"Michael, pioneers had covered wagons. Could we fix our cart like a covered wagon?" Joe asked.

"Yes, let's do that," David added.

"I don't see how we can," Michael said after a pause.

"Like we made our covered wagons at school—for the pioneer display," David suggested. "We put wheels on a box that time. Our cart looks like a box. Then we put one end of a twig in the left corner and the other end in the right corner of the front. That made a loop. We made another loop in the back and put a white cloth over it."

"There are willows here for loops," Michael said, "but what could we use for a cover?"

"We can use Mom's cotton blanket," Linda offered. "It's kind of gray-looking, but the pioneers didn't have white covered wagons anyway. They were gray. Don't let anybody tear it."

Michael and Joe went to find willows. "We'll make four loops," Michael decided. "That'll make it stronger."

They cut long, thick willow whips and returned to camp. The two boys placed the whips in curves over the cart and fastened them on with some old wire Joe found down by the creek. Then they draped the cotton blanket over the loops, and Linda folded the ends around the willow loops and sewed them.

"It looks fine!" David exclaimed.

Red growled.

"He doesn't like it. It doesn't seem like home," Linda said.

"Come on. Let's go to bed," Michael ordered. "It's four or five miles to Cheqasa. We have to get there by ten tomorrow."

He rolled up in his blanket and stared at the stars, wondering if it could be possible they were now only 40 miles from Petersburg. They had come about halfway.

Then he wondered where the night had disappeared to, for the sun peeked through the trees instead of the moon. He quickly woke everybody up.

Michael milked Nanny and tied her to the back of the cart. Betty secured Goldie's string to the cart. The little hen perched on the backboard, gazing at the goat with her little beady eyes. Red bounced around through the trees and down to the creek for a drink, barking a happy yip now and then.

The children had the rest of Mrs. Randall's bread and cookies with milk. Then each one rinsed his tin cup out in the creek. Linda packed them in the red kettle and arranged everything in the cart.

Michael patted Jake on the shoulder as they started out. "You aren't even limping. All you needed was a rest."

Betty decided to walk and let David ride because of his foot.

"But it's all right now," he insisted.

"You ride for a while, David," Linda suggested, "and when Betty gets tired you can walk."

It seemed to Michael like the longest four or five miles they had covered on the whole trip. He wanted to hurry, and of course no one could speed up Jake. Soon everyone became hungry, and the sun shone at its hottest. He had never seen so much traffic on an old road or had to get out of the way of so many cars or yell at everyone to be careful so many times. Sometimes he wondered why the oldest one had to be the boss. He wouldn't let Mother down, though. Somebody had to lead.

People went by laughing and waving. One person stuck his head out of a car and yelled, "On to Oregon."

Still Michael didn't mind the people. They were having a good time. It was a celebration.

Finally they came to a little store. Michael and Linda went in and bought food with the two dollars he had earned the day before. They had cheese sandwiches as they traveled.

Soon they found themselves in the early West. Everyone was dressed in costume. Trappers, cowboys, miners, and homesteaders mingled with one another. The women wore dresses that reached to their ankles and sunbonnets to match. Everyone rushed somewhere and yelled greetings to friends.

A boy, Michael's age, on a bicycle decorated with crepe paper stopped by them. "Are you going to be in the parade?" he asked.

"Yes. Where is it starting?"

The boy got off his bike and pushed it while talking to him. "It's a couple of blocks up the street. Supposed to start in 20 minutes. It always takes longer, though. Boy! You have some outfit! How'd you ever think this up? You'll be the best ones in the parade."

Michael straightened up proudly as he walked with his new friend.

"My name's Rusty," the boy continued. "I guess you know why. My hair isn't quite red, just rusty. What's your name?"

Michael introduced himself, and Rusty took him to the man in charge of the children's parade. His name was Mr. Ripples. That was a good name for him, Michael thought, because he was quite fat, and he laughed all the time.

"Well! Well! Rusty! What'd you bring in? A family

of pioneers! Did they get lost on the desert? You just made the fort in time. The Indians are after you!" Mr. Ripples joked.

He placed the children in line, and David yelled from the cart, "Michael, there *are* Indians behind us!" Michael turned and saw six boys dressed in feathered warbonnets, and little else besides war paint, yelling and making warlike movements with their hatchets.

"Those old Indians are going to scare Goldie," Betty complained.

Mr. Ripples blew his whistle for everyone to listen. "Now we're going to start in about five minutes. Everybody get ready. The ones in front know where to go, and I'm with them, so just follow the leader."

Quickly Michael fixed some of their things in front of the cart so David and Betty could sit and see everything. "Now, Joe, your job is to see that Red behaves. He's liable to start something. You know, fight with another dog or just plain bark too much."

"Don't you worry, Michael. I'll take care of old Red."

"Linda, you lead Nanny by her rope. If she's tied to the cart she might get excited and pull it over. I'll take care of Jake."

"And I'll take care of Goldie," Betty added.

"I'll take care of Betty," David laughed.

"OK. We're ready, then," Michael announced.

They followed a group of whooping cowboys, and Indians threatened their lives from the rear. Up ahead a band of girls hummed "Yankee Doodle" on paper-covered combs. A rhythm band with a toy snare drum, clappers, and castanets played loudly from somewhere. Rusty and some other boys weaved back and forth now and then on their bicycles to see how everyone was doing.

Michael watched first one and then the other of his family. He hoped it worked. If no one asked the wrong questions, if the cart didn't break down, if one of the children didn't get lost, or if Jake didn't balk, they just might get through.

Chapter Seven

I t was time for the parade to start, and Michael quickly surveyed his outfit. They looked like pioneers all right, since they were traveling in a covered wagon, and pioneers always had animals with them. Pioneers had big families too.

The long procession started out. After the first block, Betty peeked from the cart. "Michael, I can't see very well. May I ride Jake?"

"OK," he agreed, and helped her on Jake's back.

"Now please hand Goldie to me. She can't see either." The chicken settled down behind Betty, her bright eyes staring out at the crowd.

Just then Red yipped excitedly at the wild Indians behind them. He darted at first one and then the other. The Indians responded with loud war whoops, making the dog bark more then ever.

Trying to stop the animal from barking, Joe yelled, "Red, Red!" and raced after him. The dog circled the Indians, and Joe caught him in front of the cart. Putting his arm around Red's neck, Joe whispered softly, "Red, behave. You've got to act nice, or we can't get through this old town. We have to keep things from Mom so she'll get well. Be good, Red."

With a sigh of relief Michael saw that Joe had the dog

quieted down. They went another two blocks and a half. People kept exclaiming, "Look at the little girl and the hen on the donkey's back. See the nice dog. They even have a goat."

Everything was going fine. The children started enjoying the whole thing. Michael bowed to the watching people, and Betty waved.

Then Jake laid back his ears. Michael's heart skipped a beat. It was a bad sign. Any time the donkey's ears went back, he usually brayed in a horrible way that frightened people out of their wits. Then he'd balk. Anything might happen.

There went the hee-haw. Jake's ears pointed straight back now, his mouth stretched open, and his lips curled out. Suddenly he sat down on his hindquarters. The cart jerked forward, the front end banging on the pavement with a thud as the back end rose up in the air. David slid out of the cart. The white pail and the red kettle rolled out on the street, spilling the tin cups with a bang and a rattle.

"Michael!" Betty cried as she and Goldie slid down Jake's back. The chicken ran between people's legs, making frightened ca-ca-ca noises. Linda dropped Nanny's rope and ran after the hen, calling, "Goldie, Goldie, come back."

The Indians circled around the cart dancing wildly, and Red started barking again. The parade bumped to a halt.

Michael tried to stop Linda, but she couldn't hear him. He had seen her drop Nanny's rope, so he ran toward the goat, yelling, "Don't anybody leave the cart. Joe, hang onto Betty. Don't just sit there, David. Get up."

Although Michael looked up and down the street, he

couldn't see Nanny. She had disappeared when he was shouting instructions to the others.

A truck drove up with Mr. Ripples on the back. "Everybody stay in line a few minutes," Mr. Ripples announced into his megaphone. "The pioneers are being attacked by wild Indians, and they're having many hardships."

When Michael picked up the white pail and red kettle, he could find only four cups at first.

"I'm going to help Linda find Goldie," Betty exclaimed. Jerking free from Joe's hand, she ran between people in the crowd.

Frantic, Michael feared that Betty might get lost. It wasn't fun being the oldest and the head of the family, especially in a parade.

As the Indians calmed down, Linda returned without the hen. "I can't find her," she wailed.

Michael frowned. "You let Nanny get away. Now stay with this cart and don't leave and don't let Joe and David leave, understand? Betty ran away to look for Goldie. She'll get lost in this crowd. I'm going to look for her."

Darting here and there through the crowd, Michael shouted Betty's name, but she didn't answer. "That Jake, he would pull a stunt like this," he thought.

"Betty, Betty," he called again.

He was getting more frightened. What if he couldn't find her, and what if she got trampled in the crowd? Then a horrible thought came to him. They weren't that far from home if you didn't have to walk. Maybe Uncle Cecil was here. He might get Betty.

"Help me, God," he pleaded.

Maybe she had gone back to the cart. On his way back he spotted Mr. Ripples pushing through the crowd with Betty in his arms. She was crying, "I have to find Goldie." Michael took his sister from Mr. Ripples and held onto her hand.

"Don't worry about your hen," Mr. Ripples said. "I'll announce it from the truck." He climbed on his truck and held his megaphone up to his mouth. "Everybody watch for the little banty hen that escaped from the pioneer family. She's got a string on one leg, so if you're careful, you can catch her."

After the announcement Jake decided to get up. Everything slid from the front of the cart toward the back. Michael straightened them neatly.

Finished, he noticed Jake's ears were now straight. He knew Jake wouldn't stop again. If Nanny and Goldie would only come back.

The comb orchestra played, "You're in the Army Now," and the parade started again.

Joe and David searched the crowd for the lost animals as they walked along. Betty called from her perch on Jake's back, "Linda, do you really think someone will find Goldie? We can't leave her. She wants to be with me. I know she does."

"Don't worry," Linda consoled her. "When we get through town Michael and I'll come back and find Nanny and Goldie."

Suddenly Betty shouted, "Linda! Michael! Look! Here comes Nanny."

"Betty, sit down," Michael ordered sternly. He turned to where the girl had pointed. The goat ran toward them with a big basket in her mouth. It was a woman's purse, with artificial flowers on top of it for decorations.

"Oh, no!" he groaned.

A large woman chased Nanny from one side of the street to the other. A little short man was trying to keep up from behind.

"Michael, she's got that gleam in her eye!" Linda exclaimed.

"She'll eat the flowers," David cried.

"Don't anybody leave this cart," Michael ordered. "Joe, hold Jake's line. I'll get Nanny." He ran in front of the goat and grabbed her rope.

"Get that goat!" the woman screamed. "Stop her! She's a purse snatcher. She snatched my purse and ran off with it!"

When Nanny saw Michael in front of her, she stopped, shaking her head back and forth until the flowers looked as if they would fall off the purse.

Taking Nanny's rope, he pulled her close to him as the woman and man caught up.

"The purse snatcher! Give me my purse!" the woman demanded.

The man's face was red, and he was puffing so much he couldn't say a word.

While the crowd laughed, Michael pried the animal's mouth open and yanked the purse away from her. Handing it to the woman, he said, "I'm sorry. Nanny always gets excited when she sees anything made of straw. She thinks it's good to eat. I hope she didn't lose anything."

The woman grabbed the purse from Michael and opened it, checking all the contents. "Everything's here, but they shouldn't allow thieving goats to run around loose."

"She didn't know any better," Michael tried to explain. "That's the way goats are."

"Humph!" The woman snorted and disappeared into the crowd, with the little man still following her.

Michael tied Nanny to the back of the cart. "Now don't get into mischief again or jerk on this cart. You be a lady from now on."

"Everybody's here but Goldie," Betty cried. "I want my Goldie."

"Don't cry, honey," Linda reassured her. "We'll find her after the parade."

Joe and David walked beside Betty, talking to her. "They're trying to keep her from thinking about Goldie," Linda told Michael.

"Look, Michael!" David pointed. "We're at the fairgrounds."

"Goldie! Goldie!" screamed Betty as she slid off Jake's back and ran ahead.

When Michael looked up, he saw Red chasing Goldie toward them. Every time she turned to go the wrong way, Red headed her off, barking and nipping at her tail feathers. The little hen protested with excited ca-ca-ca-ca-ca's.

"Here, Goldie, here, dear Goldie," Betty crooned, squatting down as they came nearer.

Goldie ran straight to Betty and flapped into her arms. The dog stood waving his long red tail, his mouth open and his tongue hanging out as if to say, "Well, I rounded that one up."

"Good dog! Good old dog! Good Red," Joe and David praised him.

"Now we're all together again," Betty said, holding Goldie close as she climbed on Jake's back with a helpful push from David. "Goldie, dear, I thought you were lost. Michael said he'd never look for you, but he changed his mind. You're here! He won't have to look now. Red found you."

All the children in the parade followed the leader down the street and into the fairgrounds.

The truck stopped. Mr. Ripples stood on the truck platform. "Now I want all you cowboys, miners, trappers, and wild Indians to be quiet for a while," he announced through his megaphone. "These three men up here with me are the judges of the parade, and we want you to hear everything." Everyone became silent while he introduced the judges.

Mr. Ripples looked down at Michael. "Well, here's the pioneer family. Glad to see you made it and are all together after that long trip down the streets of Cheqasa. Which one's the leader?"

"Michael's head of the family," Linda volunteered.

"Michael, hold your hand out, and I'll help you up here by me." The boy walked over to the truck and extended his hand to Mr. Ripples, who pulled him onto the truck.

"What's your name, son?"

"Michael Larkin."

"Michael, the judges of the parade decided that your pioneer family really showed the spirit of the West. We want to give you first prize. First prize is a portable radio, just right for your room, but we thought perhaps you'd rather have the money instead of the radio because there are five of you. Then you could divide it."

The boy stared at the radio in the man's hand. It was a beautiful brown color with gold knobs. "Which one will you choose, the radio or money?"

Michael's heart seemed to be thumping in his throat. They had made it through Cheqasa, had won first prize, and could have either the radio or money. He knew which he would choose, but he'd better talk it over with the others. Quickly Mr. Ripples had the others on the truck, and they whispered among themselves.

"Have you decided?" the man asked.

"Yes," Michael answered. "We'd like very much to have the radio."

"You won't quarrel over it?" He laughed.

"No, because we won't keep it."

"What'll you do with it?"

"You see, our mother is sick. She's in a sanitarium. And she's probably lonesome without us. We'll send the radio to her, if we really won it," the boy explained.

"You won the radio. I think that's a fine thing to do with it. I know your mother will be very proud of you and the radio. Would you like to have me take it to her? I'll just leave it in the office and they can give it to her."

"Sure would!" Michael exclaimed.

Mr. Ripples handed Michael an envelope. "You write the address down, and I'll take care of everything. Of course you children will have to write a letter. You want her to know where it came from and everything."

Michael printed the address on the envelope and handed it back. "Thank you for the radio. It's a fine prize."

"Mother will think it's beautiful," Linda said.

"Our mother will have a nice time playing this,"

David added, and Joe nodded.

"It is the nicest radio," sighed Betty.

The children thanked him again, and Mr. Ripples replied, "You're welcome. I'm glad a bunch of pioneers like you got the prize."

The man helped them off the truck and spoke through his megaphone to the other children. "Everybody that entered the parade gets tickets for the carnival. Line up right over here, and I'll hand them out to you."

While the rest of the parade group were getting tickets, the Larkin children headed out to the old road. They kept quiet until they got well on their way past all the houses. Then Linda said, "We made it."

"Yes," Michael answered, "we made it, but I'm scairt. I'm more scairt than I've been on the whole trip."

"Whatever for?"

"We're over half way there. We're getting nearer. I'm scairt to face Grandma. What's she going to say when she sees us? She's liable to be really upset about what we've done."

"Yeah," the children groaned together.

"Besides . . ."

"Besides what?" all asked.

"I told Mr. Ripples our name and Mom's address. It'll be in the paper. If Uncle Cecil reads the paper, it won't take him much more than an hour to get here."

"Well, it won't be in the paper until tomorrow," Linda said. "Maybe he won't read it anyway."

"That's right," Michael agreed. "If he wasn't here and didn't see us, we're safe for a while."

"Remember the angel guards," David reminded them.

Chapter Eight

After the parade through Cheqasa, Michael and Linda were still talking about how upset Grandma would be when they arrived. "We might as well forget about it until then," she said. "It's not doing one bit of good worrying about it. We did what we thought was best."

"You're right," he agreed. "And I still think we're doing the right thing."

Betty turned around on Jake's back, facing the cart as they jogged along. She reached over and patted Goldie, who perched near Jake's tail, her small beady eyes glistening in the sun. "Goldie, I think we did the right thing, too, but you know what I wish, Goldie? I wish I could climb into bed with Mom. Wouldn't that be nice? I'd cuddle up and have Mom hug me close. She'd call me a sweet child. I'll be glad when we get to Grandma's and I'll be glad when Mom gets well. Then we'll be together again."

She sighed deeply and called down to Michael, who led Jake off the road as a car passed. "Michael, I thought we were going to travel on the beach now."

"We will soon. Joe and David're looking for a road to the beach. Why don't you walk here? Goldie can find some bugs."

Betty lay on her tummy across Jake's back and slid feetfirst to the ground. Michael lifted the hen into some tall weeds. She pecked and scratched, making contented sounds when she found an insect. "Eat lots, Goldie, dear," Betty murmured as she sat down in the dry grass.

Red ran back and forth from the cart to see if Betty was all right. "I'm fine," she told him. "You don't need to make such a fuss. Goldie's eating her dinner. I have to wait for her."

The dog looked at her and wagged his tail.

"You might as well sit down," Betty said. "Be nice and quiet. You mustn't bother Goldie. She'll lay an egg after while."

The dog sat down and gazed at the rest of the children up the road. Suddenly, from nowhere it seemed to Betty, a tall boy was standing by her. Red growled. She put her hand on his head as she stood up. The animal quieted down, waiting to see what he should do.

Betty looked up at the boy. *He's taller than Michael,* she thought, *but dressed about the same. Blue jeans and a striped shirt. But he's different. Has very dark eyes, maybe they're black. His hair is black and straight. His skin is dark too.*

When he smiled, she decided not to be afraid. "I'm letting Goldie eat her dinner. The rest of us are ahead with Jake, our donkey."

"Are you taking Goldie to the beach?" the boy asked.

"Yes. When we find a road down there we're going to travel two days on the beach."

"What's your name?"

"Betty."

"Mine is Rick. There's a road just ahead to the beach. Will you do something for me when you get there?"

"If I can. I'm not very big."

"You don't need to be big," he smiled. "My family's camped a ways down the beach. We're Indians. My father, my mother, three sisters, two brothers, and grandfather. Grandfather is very old. He's like his people long ago. Life is different now, so I must help Grandfather. If I help him he can pretend and make things up. I buy some things for him that he would have made long ago. He needs this to make him happy. He calls it his secret."

Rick held a small bag with a drawstring at the top of it. It looked like Mr. Smith's suede jacket.

"After I buy the secret, he keeps it in this bag. Please, Betty, take this to the old man. He needs it to be happy."

"Why don't you take it?"

Rick pointed to some brick buildings off to the left. "That's an Indian school. I'm working there this summer so I can go to school in September. It's against the rules to leave. That's why I'm not with my family. It's the first time I haven't gone fishing and crabbing with them. If you're going to walk on the beach two days, you will come to their camp. Of course you will have to go back to a trail or the road once in awhile because you can't always travel on the beach and get by the big rocks and logs. But I don't think you'll miss my family. Will you take it?"

"I guess so," Betty replied, "but I'm afraid of Indians."

Handing her the bag, Rick laughed. "Are you afraid of me?"

"No, but you're like Michael, my big brother, except you're dark."

"My family and I are alike. Grandfather is the only different one. He's very kind. Please, it's important. Grandfather likes to pretend that it's like the old days.

Don't tell your family about it. It's a secret. When you give it to Grandfather, he will give you a present."

"How do you know?"

"Because I know Grandfather. Will you, Betty?"

"I'll try. I'll try very hard to make Grandfather Indian happy." Betty smiled.

"Thank you, Betty," Rick said. "Good-bye."

Betty watched him disappear down the road, then wondered what was in the little bag, but she didn't open it. The grandfather Indian called it his secret. She rubbed the soft bag with her hand. "It's a secret," she whispered. "I mustn't tell. It will make Grandfather Indian happy."

Picking Goldie up, she ran with Red to catch up with the others. She slipped into the back of the cart, and when no one was looking, she put the bag into her coat pocket.

Linda led Nanny through the grass, stopping now and then to let the goat nibble a bit. "Who were you talking to?" she asked.

Betty thought about the secret in her coat pocket and about Rick. "An Indian boy, but I wasn't afraid. He's just like Michael, only dark."

"Of course." Linda laughed.

"I'll be glad when we get to the beach. I'm hungry."

"It won't be long," Linda smiled. "It'll be nice there. We won't have to worry about cars. Michael says we can have dinner and play on the beach the rest of the day, because we're ahead of schedule."

"What's a schedule?" Betty asked.

"Well, if you plan on getting somewhere at a certain time, that's your schedule. If you get there ahead of the time you planned, you're ahead of schedule."

"Linda, I wish Mom would get well ahead of schedule and be at Grandma's when we get there."

"Wouldn't that be nice!" Linda agreed. "We all miss Mom. I guess you miss her more than any of us."

Just then Joe and David came bounding over a little hill to the right, yelling, "You can get to the beach right here. Hurry, Michael."

They guided Jake over an old road that led to the beach. "We must be careful and stay away from deep, dry sand, or we'll get stuck," Michael warned.

"Is it all right if we take our shoes off?" Joe asked. "These old things of David's aren't shoes anyway."

"We'd better all take our shoes off," Michael replied. "They'll get wet and full of sand if we leave them on." The children stowed their shoes in the cart.

They followed the beach until they came to a huge pile of driftwood washed up against a high bank. Michael tied Jake to a log, and Linda secured Nanny to a little scrub tree. Betty fastened Goldie's string to the cart near some weeds along the bank. Then the children ran to the water, chasing the waves out and running back so they wouldn't get splashed. Red raced back and forth, barking at the waves. Then they looked for shells and put some in the cart for their grandmother.

"Let's build a fire," Michael suggested.

"Yes, we can roast the potatoes we bought in Cheqasa," Linda said. It wasn't long until they had a big campfire made of driftwood.

"The fire feels good," Betty said.

"Yes," Linda agreed, "it's getting cold down here. The wind sure is blowing." After Betty got tired of warming herself, she walked to the end of a big pile of driftwood. She liked watching the seagulls fly and the tiny little birds run in the sand. The dog came bounding up to her, and the birds flew away. "Shame on you, Red. You frightened my little birdies. Let's go back to the fire."

Everyone grew quiet as they waited for the potatoes, all thinking their own thoughts as they watched the dancing flames of the fire. Soon they pulled the hard black coats from the potatoes and salted them. They had a little milk and some cheese left over from their lunch to go with the potatoes.

After they had everything packed away, Linda said, "Michael, let's not stay close to the beach tonight. It's getting cold, and the tide might come this far."

"I was thinking the same thing. Why don't we go a ways before it gets dark? We can head up toward the road."

"Fine. It seems lonesome down here, especially since we put the fire out. There's not a soul around, only the ocean."

Betty put her hand in Linda's. It did seem lonesome, and she was cold.

As the wind grew chillier, one by one the children went to the cart and got their coats. Linda was fastening Betty's top button when they heard loud rumblings in the sky. "Thunder!" Michael exclaimed. "It's going to rain."

Big ploppy drops started falling, the wind behind pushing them. It was getting darker too. "What will we do, Linda?" Betty wailed. "I'm getting all wet."

"We'll have to hurry. I don't know where we'll go. Our blankets are getting soaked."

"We could go to that haunted house," David suggested.

"Don't be silly. There isn't a house down here, especially a haunted one."

"Yes, there is," Joe argued, pointing. "It's up there and over that way, past those rocks. David and I found it when we came down here the first time looking for the road."

"We're not going to a haunted house, are we?" Betty begged. "I'd rather freeze and soak."

"No, dear," Linda said. "We won't go to a haunted house because there isn't any such thing. That's just a story."

"Is there anybody living near the house?" Michael inquired.

"Nobody lives in it or around it," David answered. "But I think ghosts stay there at night. It looks like a haunted house."

"You boys are ridiculous," Michael said. "You know that isn't true. Let's hurry. Maybe we can get inside until it stops raining."

Michael flipped Jake's reins, and for once he hurried. David and Joe led the way through the now-dark night. Betty wondered if they would miss the Indian family's camp. She felt the secret in her pocket. Betty didn't like to have a secret from the others. She would rather talk about it with them. But she mustn't. Rick said it was important not to tell, and she must make Grandfather Indian happy. He could pretend to everybody he had made what was in the little bag.

"Here it is," Joe announced at last.

"It's been empty a long time," Michael yelled above the noise of the wind and rain. "There aren't any doors or windows. Let's go in."

It was a big two-story house. The wind whistled

through the open windows and doors, but it was dry in the middle of the room.

"We can't leave Nanny and Jake out in the rain," Michael said. "Why don't we bring them inside? After all, it's an old place. They won't hurt anything."

"Let's do," Linda replied. "It won't be nearly as lonesome."

The boys soon had Nanny and Jake standing in the front room. David laughed. "All the family's in now but Goldie."

"Where's Goldie?" Betty wanted to know.

"She's all right," Michael reassured her. "She's in the cart. I'm going to see if I can put it in that shed out back. The door opening looks wide enough. You boys come and help me." They pulled the cart into the shed, and none too soon, for the rain was turning into a real storm.

Michael carried Goldie to Betty. She perched the little hen on an old box.

"I wish we had a fire," Linda said.

"There's a stove in the kitchen," Joe informed them. "Maybe we could build a fire in it."

All the children followed him into the kitchen. "It's a big old range. The stovepipe looks OK," Michael observed. "Doesn't seem to be anything wrong with the chimney."

They gathered up old boards and boxes. It took quite a bit of coaxing, but they finally got a good fire burning.

"We'll have this room, and the animals can have the front room," Linda decided. They took the blankets out of the cart and hung them around the stove to dry.

"There's a bed upstairs," David said. "I wouldn't sleep there, of course. I think that's where the ghosts stay."

"No more of that ghost business," Linda scolded.

"Anyway, we'll sleep close to the stove. We can keep warm then."

They made their beds on the floor. The blankets didn't get too dry, but the children were tired and didn't want to wait any longer. "It's hard," Joe complained, trying to find a comfortable position to lie in. No one answered, for they were all thinking the same thing.

Betty cuddled up close to Linda and clung to her hand. Frightened, she wondered if there were any ghosts. Maybe Michael and Linda didn't know about such things. She could hear many creepy sounds.

"Are the angel guards stronger than ghosts?" Betty asked Linda.

"Of course. If there is anything around, Jesus will send a host of angel guards to take care of us. We'll pray before we go to sleep."

Chapter Nine

Suddenly Betty sat up and looked around in the dark. Oh! She knew now. They had come to the beach, and it had started raining. Then they had built a fire in an old house. Joe and David said it was haunted. She could hear the ghosts crying.

"Linda," she whispered. "Linda, the ghosts are here."

Linda, David, and Joe all raised up from the floor at the same time. "That's them," Joe cried. "I knew it. Let's get out of here. Michael, Michael! They're wailing. Let's go quick!"

Michael raised up. "What's all the fuss about?"

"Hear that awful noise?" Linda whispered.

"I don't hear a thing," he grumbled.

"There it is," David exclaimed. "They're awful sad. It's dangerous when they're sad like that."

Betty tried to be brave, but she couldn't help clutching Linda's arm tightly when the wailing noise floated around again.

"It's shivery," Joe said hoarsely.

Quickly Michael started putting his shoes on. "Come on, everybody. I can't sleep with all this crying about ghosts. We might as well get going. It's quit raining anyway."

Each child rolled up his things and put them into the cart. The boys pushed the cart outside while Linda let

Jake and Nanny out and Betty carried Goldie. Red frolicked around as if nothing were wrong. They hitched the donkey up, and as they left, a long melancholy sound quivered through the air.

Without saying a word, they hurried over among some short bushy trees. Later they stopped under one of them and Michael handed the blankets out to the children. Wrapping up, they huddled close together. It was too wet to lie down and too dark for traveling.

Betty's eyes felt heavy, but she didn't want to close them. She blinked several times. No, she mustn't go to sleep with ghosts around. The boys were soon dozing. She was going to stay awake, though.

"Are you asleep?" she whispered to Linda.

"No, and don't worry. Everything will be all right. Just think about your Bible verses. God promises to take care of us."

Eventually, Betty went to sleep after all. When she woke up she glanced around. Everybody seemed all right. Goldie strutted around, and Nanny munched on some grass. "The sun's coming," she said quietly.

"Yes," Linda answered.

"I can see the house. I guess the ghosts are gone."

The girls stood up. "That's an apple tree by the house," Linda said. "I wonder if it has any apples on it."

"Look at all the birds!" Betty exclaimed. "They're having a meeting in the apple tree. One's a blue jay."

The boys rubbed their eyes and stretched. "I see two flickers," David said.

"They're sure noisy," Michael commented. "They're after something."

"See a little owl sitting in the hollow of the tree," Joe said. "The owl's glaring at the others. I think they're after him."

"He probably stole their eggs," Michael told them.

A sad, mournful wail floated down from the apple tree, and the owl flew away, the other birds scolding as he left. The children looked at each other in astonishment. "The owl made that awful noise last night," Linda finally said. "It's not scary when you know where it comes from."

"Some ghost," Michael muttered in disgust. "Just a little old screech owl."

The twins doubled up in laughter. "Owls are ghosts," they yelled. "Did you know that owls are ghosts?"

"I don't think it's funny," Betty protested. .

"I don't either," Linda said. "But I do think there are apples on that tree. Let's get some while Michael milks Nanny."

David and Joe climbed the scraggly old apple tree and shook the limbs. Little apples came tumbling down on the ground. The children ate all they wanted and filled the red kettle and their arms. "They're not very big, but they're good," Michael said as he bit into one they brought to him.

"Let's drink our milk and get going," he said a couple of minutes later, tossing his apple core as far as he could up in the air. "We'll travel along the beach as long as we can. People won't wonder about us down here, mostly because not many come here."

Later they had to leave the beach and follow a bumpy trail because the cart couldn't get by some huge rocks and piles of driftwood. They were glad when they could return to the beach. Betty picked up a few shells, but no one seemed interested in them. "I guess we're lonesome to see our mom," she sighed.

"Yeah," Michael agreed. "It's really not much fun to be your own boss."

Instead of halting for lunch, they ate the little apples as they traveled. During the afternoon David and Joe ran ahead and didn't come back for a long time. "I hope David and Joe aren't stirring up any more ghosts," Linda said after awhile.

Michael laughed. "Me too."

Suddenly the boys appeared from over a sand dune, yelling loudly. Red raced along, waving his long tail and yipping with excitement.

"If it's any more ghost owls, I won't listen," grumbled Betty.

As the boys came closer, they could hear them shout, "Indians! Indians! Indians up there. Tepees and everything!"

"That does it," Michael said. "I'm getting tired of their stories."

Betty slipped her hand in her pocket and rubbed the little suede bag. Grandfather Indian must be ahead, and she'd make him happy when they got there.

Joe skidded in the sand about three feet before he stopped in front of Jake. David bumped into him from behind. No one could understand a word they were saying until Michael ordered, "Now stop. Be quiet. Think! Then tell us what you're talking about. If it's some wild yarn, I'm going to whop you. So be careful what you say."

"It's Grandfather Indian," Betty said.

Linda and Michael didn't hear her because they were listening to Joe. "I think they're friendly Indians.

We saw three tepees, and they have a big campfire. There are a lot of kids running around and an old man with two long pigtails like Linda's."

"Did you talk to them?" Michael asked.

"No, we hid behind a sand dune and watched," David said. "You never can tell about Indians. They might scalp us, especially that old man. He's just like in pictures."

"Those Indians are camping down there. They won't bother us," Michael reassured the children.

"We can't go around them," Joe explained. "There are scrub trees, real thick, behind their camp, and the tide's coming in now."

"It's all right. Indians are friendly. They aren't like the old days," Michael explained.

Eager to reach the Indian camp, the children chattered to each other and encouraged Jake and Nanny over the hard-packed sand. But to their disappointment, when they came to the tepees no one seemed to be about. They didn't want to be questioned, but it would have been nice to have seen the Indian family.

Betty didn't know what to do. Rick had told her not to tell her family about the secret. He was afraid it would not be a secret if she mentioned it. Now the grandfather Indian wasn't here. What should she do? She walked slower and slower as they passed the camp, until the others were ahead of her.

Then she stopped and gazed at the tepees. She saw poles arranged in a circle, with the ends crossed at the top and a canvas wrapped around the poles to make a shelter.

"They aren't made of animal skins, Little One, and they aren't made from the bark of trees. The ways of the white man are easier. All we have to do now is go to the store and buy."

Betty glanced up at the Indian man who had appeared by her. Old and stooped, his face looked like leather with dents in it. He had long gray pigtails and wore faded blue jeans and a navy blue shirt with big white polka dots. The man had a big red handkerchief folded into a band and tied around his head.

Betty liked his suede moccasins. She smiled up at him. "Are you Grandfather Indian?"

The old man grunted slightly. "I've many grandchildren."

"Is Rick you grandson?"

"Rick's my grandson. Rick's a good grandson. Too bad Rick's gone. Always he's with us on my birthday feast until this time."

"Here, Grandfather Indian," Betty said, holding the little suede pouch up to the old man. "Rick sent this."

The old Indian clutched the pouch to his heart. "Rick not forget. Rick and I always pretend to others that secret is made Indian way, but Rick buy for me, much easier. Others know we buy, but all pretend."

"Goodbye, Grandfather Indian. I must catch up with the others."

"Wait! You stay. Call back the others. Stay for birthday feast."

Betty started to call, but the other children had already returned. The grandfather asked all of them their names and where they were going. Michael explained to him that they were going to live with their grandmother.

"Good white children, know how to get along very well by self," the Indian commented. "Good you can do that."

Soon Rick's mother and father and many children showed up, carrying salmon. The grandfather waved the little suede bag at them. "See! Secret! Little white girl bring from Rick."

"That's what you were up to," Linda said to Betty. "What's in the bag?"

"I don't know. It's a secret."

Rick's parents smiled at the children and said that of course they must stay for the feast. The grandfather would be very unhappy if they didn't.

Michael staked Jake and Nanny out near the scrub trees and tied Goldie to the cart. Then the boys went with the Indian boys, exploring in the trees. There was a little girl Betty's age, one Linda's age, and another older than Linda.

Betty liked the Indian family. The grandfather Indian was the only one with pigtails. The others looked and acted much like any other people the children knew.

The girls helped prepare the food. They wrapped huge pieces of salmon in seaweed and placed them deep in the coals of the fire to bake. The mother made corn bread and baked it in a big, heavy Dutch oven. Betty thought it was funny for Indians to use a Dutch oven. It resembled an iron kettle, and they placed it on the coals, heaping more coals on top of it.

She and Pearl, the little girl her age, went with the grandfather through tall grass and around logs to a creek. In between some rocks lying in the cold water rested two big green watermelons.

"For the feast," he said as he stooped over and pulled

the watermelons upon the grass. He carried one under each arm as they started back.

The boys met them on the path. Betty stared at them. They were both smaller than Michael and looked like Rick except that they were younger.

When they returned to camp, it was getting dark. The other girls and Linda were spreading a big piece of canvas out on the ground. Rick's mother set the baked salmon and vegetables on the cloth. His father took the corn bread out of the Dutch oven. They left the huge piles of baked potatoes near the fire.

Grandfather Indian stood at one end of the canvas table, and the others all sat down. He gazed up in the sky and talked in his language a long time. Betty decided he was saying grace the Indian way.

The children were hungry, and the food tasted good. The Indian family didn't question them because they didn't eat the salmon. If they had, Linda was ready to tell them her mother believed vegetables, grains, and fruits were best for the body.

After everyone had eaten all he could and the things were cleared away, the grandfather said, "Now the surprise."

He went into one of the tepees. When he returned, he had on new beaded moccasins and a short beaded thing that looked like a shirt. His pants and sleeves had fringes on them. He had a headband with beautiful feathers on it, and his face was painted. In his hand he held the little suede pouch Betty had brought him.

Clearing a smooth place on the ground with his foot, he pulled many capsules out of the little pouch. Each capsule contained different colored sand. He glanced up at

Betty. "See what Rick buy. Indian way hard."

In the flickering light of the campfire everyone watched him closely as he opened and spread the different colors in a beautiful design on the hard ground. Betty studied the design one way, and it looked like the sun and moon and many stars. She walked around and stared at it from another angle. It seemed to be a beautiful colored bird. From whatever side she looked the picture appeared different.

The Indian family sat in a wide circle around the design and motioned the children to do the same. Some of them pounded sticks together, and others clapped their hands in rhythm while the grandfather danced around the design on the ground. He stooped low and went through all types of imaginary actions as if he were fighting with different animals.

One of the Indian boys whispered, "Grandfather was chief far to the south and knows about many dances and their meanings. Some of them he even makes up. He always does the dance with the colored sand picture on his birthday for us. He would be very unhappy if he couldn't because it makes him think of the old days and his ancestors."

Betty felt pleased because she had helped make him happy.

After his dance the grandfather gathered all the children in a circle and taught them another dance. It was fun. They stooped way over and did a little hop. Once in a while he gave what he called a big Indian war whoop. "Now it is all a game," he said. "In past years it was very important."

Before they went to bed, the grandfather said to Betty, "In the morning I will have a surprise for you."

Chapter Ten

The children made their camp near the Indian family. "It's nice to be by other people at night," Linda commented before they dropped off to sleep.

In the morning they had breakfast with their Indian friends, packed the cart, and started on.

"Wait," the grandfather said. He went into his tepee and brought something to Betty. "Your surprise," he said, handing it to her.

"Oh! Oh!" Betty exclaimed. "Moccasins, just like yours. They're soft like the little bag. Beau-ti-ful beads on them. Thank you, Grandfather Indian."

He patted her shoulder. "Made after feast. Good girl—made birthday feast happy."

She took his hand. "I'll never forget you, Grandfather Indian." Carefully she put the moccasins in the cart where they wouldn't get lost.

After the children left the Indian family, they switched back and forth from an old road to the beach several times. When they stopped later, Linda ordered, "Now you boys march right out and get water. We're going to clean up all the dishes, shake the sand out of everything, and everybody's going to be clean. Tomorrow is Sabbath. Betty and I washed the other clothes yesterday."

"Aw, Linda, are you going to be bossy all day?" Joe grumbled.

"Yea," David whined.

"You can make up your mind, Mr. David and Mr. Joe, we're going to be as neat as we can be when we go through Petersburg. Mom wouldn't want us to shame Grandma by being sloppy and dirty. We want to please Jesus. There isn't anything else we can do to get ready for Sabbath. We want to have a better Sabbath than the last one."

"Might as well give up, boys," Michael sighed. "She's right. Come on, let's shake the blankets while Linda and Betty wash the cups."

"Water first," Linda demanded.

All through the water-carrying and the blanket-shaking the twins grumbled. They continued through the cleaning up. "You always agree with Linda," Joe complained. "We won't get to Grandma's today."

"That's right. Grandma lives the other side of Petersburg," David added.

"About three miles the other side," Linda told them.

"Ba-a-a," the goat objected.

"Linda, won't we get to sleep at Grandma's tonight?" Betty wailed. "Won't we, Linda, in a real bed, a soft bed?"

Linda patted her sister's shoulder. "Never mind, honey."

The little girl's face looked gloomy.

"I'm hungry!" Joe complained. "David's hungry!"

"Yeah," David echoed.

"Won't ever get to Grandma's anyway. We'll starve," Joe continued.

Michael's face turned red. "I'm hungry, too," he yelled. "But we're going to get to Grandma's before sundown. Do you understand? Come on, get your hen, Betty. Tie that goat to the cart, Joe. Round up Red. Hurry up. Get this stuff put away. We're on our way."

All the time Michael ordered them about, the children became more quiet. No one said anything until they were on the road and couldn't see the beach.

"You don't need to be so crabby, Michael," Joe said. "You're the oldest. You're the one who'll get it when we get to Grandma's."

"Yes, I'll be the one who gets it," Michael said gruffly. "I'm the oldest, and I'll get it. Then you can all laugh and be happy."

"Michael Larkin, it was my fault Nanny ate the tickets in the first place," Linda objected. "It wasn't your fault. Betty made us think of traveling this way. Joe, David, and Betty started hitching Jake before we agreed to come. You won't be blamed any more than the rest of us."

"No," Betty said, taking her oldest brother's hand. "We won't let anybody hurt you. We'll tell Grandma you're not to blame. We love you, Michael."

Goldie hopped on the front board of the cart from her place with a ca-ca-ca-dak-a.

"Goldie's laid an egg," Betty chanted three times.

Carefully Linda wrapped the egg in leaves and slipped it into one of the tin cups, saving it until there were enough for all. Michael didn't say anything, but he figured it would be five days before there'd be enough eggs for all of them, and by then they'd be at Grandma's. No use mentioning it, though. He knew everyone was tired and hungry.

Jake seemed to know they were nearing the end of

their journey. He didn't balk all morning, but walked so fast the children couldn't dally.

Then it happened. The right wheel wobbled a bit, creaked, and rolled over to the side of the road ahead of the little group. Jake stopped in his tracks.

The cart tipped over to one side, and the red kettle rolled out with five tin cups bumping after it and one broken egg leaking over the road. The blankets and other things slid out quietly in a heap. Everyone stood and stared.

Betty broke the silence by picking up some large pieces of gravel and throwing them at the wheel. "Mean old thing! Meanest thing ever! We'll never sleep at Grandma's tonight."

No one said anything.

Linda started picking up objects and putting them in a pile. Quietly the others helped. Michael rolled the wheel back to the cart and examined it. "Either the axle came out of the wheel or the wheel came off the axle. The pin that holds it on is gone."

"What pin?" Linda asked.

"See, this is the axle," he explained. "It goes through the wheel, then the pin goes through this hole on the end of the axle. That's what kept the wheel from coming off. You can call it a pin or call it a bolt. It doesn't make any difference, because it's gone."

"Maybe we can find it."

The children retraced their steps, searching here and there for the bolt, but they couldn't find it. At last they gave up and turned around. Almost back at the cart, Betty suddenly stumbled and grabbed Linda's skirt.

They both looked at the spot where her foot had been. There was the bolt.

"Is this it?" Linda asked.

Michael grabbed it. "That's it."

They gathered around the cart. The boys lifted the heavy wheel up and tried to slip it back on the axle.

"That's out," Michael stormed. "Anybody can see the axle's bent way up on the end. Some old bump did that. We can't make the wheel stay on there even if we get it back on. It would just come off again."

"We'd better get everything off the road," Linda said. "People can't get curious then."

The boys held the side of the cart without a wheel while Jake pulled it toward the trees. The one wheel rolled crooked, but they managed.

The twins staked Jake out in some grass and tied Nanny to a small sapling. They all helped carry the things, and Michael rolled the other wheel over by the cart. When it lost balance and fell over, Michael and Linda sat down on it, both automatically putting their elbows in their laps and sinking their chins into their hands.

"There's only one thing to do," Linda suggested. "Sleep on it, and then we can think better."

"Sleep," Michael sputtered, "it's not even twelve o'clock."

The other children had been investigating. They came running from across the road, Joe yelling, "Come on, bring something. We've found blackberries."

Michael grabbed the white pail, and Linda took the red kettle. They followed the others through the brush and trees until they reached a wild blackberry patch. They ate many of the berries and filled the red kettle about half full.

"There doesn't seem to be any more," Linda stated finally.

"Berries don't stop me from being hungry," David said.

In their wandering through the woods they came out quite a way up the road from their temporary camp. "Let's walk back in the field," Michael suggested, glancing around to see if anybody was watching. They crossed the road and walked through weeds and tall grass until they came to more trees.

Michael looked around. "It seems like someone must have camped here a long time ago. There's an old platform with a wall. That's to put a tent on."

"They weren't very clean campers," David remarked. "Look at the old pile of cans and stuff around here."

"Hey, Linda!" Michael exclaimed. "What kind of plants are those by the cans? Are they what I think they are?"

She studied the green plants while the other children crowded about her. "I know. They're potato vines!"

"That's right," Michael agreed, "and they have blossoms on them. They might have a few potatoes."

"I don't know," Linda said, a puzzled expression on her face. "Usually potato vines are dry and brown when people dig them. These vines are green."

"There's only one way to find out. Boys, go get the ax. That's the only thing we have to dig with. It won't make it any duller than it is."

The boys soon returned with the ax.

"I wonder how these potato vines happen to be growing here," Linda mused.

"The campers probably threw their potato peelings out with the cans. The peelings sprouted and grew. I know if you happen to leave a potato in the ground when you dig them, it sprouts and comes up the next year," Michael explained. "Mom calls these kind volunteer potatoes."

The other children squatted down, gazing fascinated while Michael dug. Every time he found a potato any larger than a marble, they screamed with excitement.

The vines had many tiny potatoes and a few about two inches across. Michael even dug two medium sized ones. They uncovered enough to fill the white pail. On the way to camp they washed them in a small stream.

"We'll build a fire," Michael said. "You can boil them in the pail, can't you, Linda?"

The children made a huge fire and could hardly wait. In spite of the hot sun they stood near the fire waiting. "A watched pot never boils," Linda said.

"This isn't a pot," David protested. "It's a pail."

Finally they had their plates loaded with tiny potatoes and blackberries and sat in the shade to eat. Every few minutes someone said, "These potatoes are sure good."

Red went from one to another, receiving a small potato at each stop.

Just as they were finishing up their dinner a large car stopped, and a man in uniform climbed out and approached them. "Are you children alone?" he asked.

Michael straightened his shoulders and stood tall. This was it, he supposed. Someone had finally come right out and asked the dreaded question. Why couldn't the old cart have lasted just one more day? If it had, they wouldn't have been here.

"Yes, we're alone," he told the man.

"What's your name?" he asked Michael.

"Michael Larkin."

"Michael Larkin, eh? Well, Michael Larkin," he said sternly, "I suppose you have a permit to build a big fire like this the last of August, in the driest part of the year, here among all these trees?"

Chapter Eleven

Michael stared up at the tall man. He knew it was August and that the country was dry, and he had heard of permits to build fires. But he had forgotten somehow about them. Twelve-year-olds probably couldn't get one anyway.

"This is the way many forest fires are started, from campfires," the ranger continued.

"We never started a forest fire," Joe defended his brother. "Michael always makes us put the fire out, and if there isn't any water, we put dirt on it. Michael wouldn't let us start a forest fire."

David edged over close to Joe. "That's right. We know better than to start a forest fire."

The man's face lost some of its sternness, and he spoke more kindly. "I'm glad to hear you're careful. Some adults aren't that careful. Let's put this out right now."

They kicked dirt over the fire in their usual way, and Michael dug dirt with the hatchet in order to have enough.

The ranger stood back watching them. "It's a good job. Where do you live, Michael?"

The boy's shoulders slumped. The cart was broken. There wasn't any use keeping anything secret. "We're going to live with our grandma. She lives about three miles the other side of Petersburg."

Just then Jake gave a loud hee-haw from the bushes where the children had staked him. As if she didn't want to be left out, Nanny gave two short baas.

"Whose animals are these?" the ranger demanded. "You aren't taking those animals with you? Where did you come from?"

Michael sighed. All hope was gone now. "We used to live the other side of Lakeview," he said. "We're going to our grandma's."

Linda gave Michael a sympathetic look and added, "Our mom was very sick. She went to the sanitarium to get well. That's why we're traveling. When Mom gets well, she's coming to live with Grandma. We had tickets to come on the train."

"Why didn't you use the tickets?" the ranger interrupted.

Betty stood in front of the ranger. "You were cranky when you came," she said. "Michael was that way when the wheel broke on our cart and when Nanny ate our train tickets and when I wanted to bring Goldie. Goldie's my banty hen. She lays eggs for us. She lays them right in the cart. Do you want to see Goldie?"

The ranger smiled at Betty, and she ran to get the hen without waiting for him to answer her. He patted Goldie's feathers and said, "What a nice hen."

"Wasn't Nanny bad? She ate our train tickets. She's most always good, though. She gives us milk to drink."

The ranger squatted down by Betty. He questioned first one of them, then another, until he had the whole story from the beginning. Then he stood up. "I think it would be a shame for you youngsters to come all this distance and not make it. You're two miles from Petersburg, and you say three miles farther is where your grandma lives. Let's take a look at that wheel. If we could fix it, you'd be in your Grandma's yard by dark."

As they stood around the cart, Michael showed the bent axle to the ranger.

"This cart is made strong. Who made it?" the man asked.

"We don't know," Michael answered. "It was on our place when we moved there."

"It goes to show, you can make things out of scraps if you try. They've used pipe for an axle. I'll see if any of my tools will help."

They followed him to his car, where he got some heavy wrenches and a large sledgehammer. "A ranger has to have all kinds of things to work with," he commented. "He never knows what he's going to need."

Pushing the cart against a log, they rested the axle on it. Then the ranger lifted the large sledgehammer high and whanged on the axle several times. It was hard to strike the axle without hitting the cart. He paused and felt it, then hammered it some more. "It looks pretty straight now," he said.

The children started chattering, and Michael examined the axle. It was quite straight again. Slipping the wheel on, they put the bolt where it belonged.

"Now get ready to go," the ranger ordered.

He stood watching while Michael hitched Jake up to the cart and had the boys tie Nanny to the back of the cart. Putting his hands on his hips, he grinned while Linda and Betty placed the red kettle, the tin cups, and the white pail, along with the blankets, in the cart. When Betty perched Goldie on Jake's back, he laughed right out loud.

"You kids couldn't possibly be the pioneers that won a prize in the Cheqasa parade? I guess not; you don't have a covered wagon. Besides, their uncle is looking for them. Says they belong to him. Their mother's in a mental hospital. He was in Petersburg looking for them yesterday. Maybe he's still there."

The ranger looked straight into Michael's eyes.

Michael flinched, but answered bravely, "Our mother is not in a mental hospital. She's in a sanitarium to rest. She worked too hard and worried too much. She instructed us to go live with Grandma Bell. That's what we're doing."

"Good," the ranger said. "You get there as fast as you can."

He followed the little outfit out to the road, then telling them to wait a minute, he took a paper bag out of his car. "Here's some lunch I was taking to some men working around here. I can get some more. You children take the lunch for later. No more fires! You understand? Absolutely none!"

"We understand," Michael assured him.

David put the paper bag into the cart, and they thanked the ranger again for helping them. The ranger slid into his car and turned it around. The children started toward Petersburg, waving at him. He stuck his head out the window and called, "Good luck."

"Same to you."

"We've got to step right along," Michael said. "It's Grandma's by dark—or Uncle Cecil's."

Chapter Twelve

They walked along quietly, each thinking about the end of their journey. However, as the hot sun bore down upon them, they began complaining about the heat again.

Finally, after everyone had grumbled for a while, Linda said, "We have the cart fixed. It's hot, but we're still on our way. Let's be thankful about that."

"Yes, but I'm hot," Betty sighed. "I can't walk any longer."

"OK, Betty," Michael told her, "come here and you may climb on with Goldie." He helped her on Jake's back. The donkey didn't even pause.

"Jake's in a hurry to get there," Linda observed. "He hasn't balked one bit today. His amble gets pretty frisky sometimes too."

Joe and David exclaimed together, "It looks like a river up ahead."

"I think we'd save time if we got cooled off," Michael suggested. "We'll swim. After all, we're only about half a mile from Petersburg."

The river turned out to be rather low due to the dry, hot weather. The children let the animals drink, then staked them out to eat. They all took their shoes off and ran into the water, splashing around in their clothes. Red followed them, and they threw sticks for him to swim after. Linda mud-crawled toward the bank.

"Your braids look like two long tails floating behind," David exclaimed.

She laughed and ducked her head under the water, but the tails still stuck out. Raising her head out of the water, she shook it like a dog.

Michael and Joe had a water fight, and Betty was in the middle of it. She splashed out of the water onto the sand. "It's raining too hard. Let's go," she cried.

Linda left the water and patted her little sister on the shoulder. "Come on, let's get the lunch the ranger gave us."

"They're getting the lunch," Joe yelled. At that announcement everyone gathered around the cart while Linda passed out sandwiches.

"There must have been five men working up there," Joe figured.

"How do you know?" David asked.

"Because there are five of us, and we each have a sandwich."

"We're wet enough to be cool," Michael said when they were through eating. "Let's go."

"Our clothes will dry straight. We won't even be very wrinkled," Linda said.

They didn't bother to go around Petersburg but decided to walk right through the little town.

"After all, if we go around," Michael reasoned, "the few people in the houses will only tell the few people in the stores. Besides, if a patrolman or a policeman asks where we're going, all we have to say is, 'Three miles out to the Bell farm.' We're already here, and that's that."

As they hesitated on a narrow road before entering the main street, a large black car hurtled by. A man with an angry expression hunched behind the steering wheel. Michael and Linda exclaimed together, "Uncle Cecil!"

The children looked frightened.

"He's in a hurry," Michael reassured them. "He isn't going our way. Don't worry."

About six o'clock Michael said, "I'm going into this farmhouse and ask how much farther it is." No one answered him. They stood waiting, too tired for conversation.

"Would you tell me how far the Bell farm is from here?" Michael asked a man in the yard.

"Around the bend, first place on the right," he answered, staring at the strange-looking outfit.

Michael thanked him and hurried back to the other children. "Right around the corner! Come on, Jake! Get up!"

Forgetting how tired they were, David and Joe raced ahead faster than they had during the whole trip. Suddenly Linda and Michael stopped and looked at each other, both thinking about the came thing.

"Well, anyway we're here, Michael. If we're going to get bawled out, we might as well get it over with. I'm still glad we're here."

By the time they reached the Bell farm, David and Joe had their grandmother out in the yard to meet them. "Grandma," Betty called, turning sideways on Jake's back and sliding on her tummy to the ground. "Grandma," she shouted again as she ran into her arms.

Linda and Michael stood back, waiting, while the white-haired woman in the pink cotton dress hugged

Betty to her and told the twins to bring the others in. The twins were so excited they didn't hear her.

"George, take the animals and cart to the barn," she called to a man on the porch. "Take good care of those animals. They're faithful old things." Red ran around her and Betty, barking and wagging his tail until she spoke to him. "Yes, you're a good dog, and you did a fine job."

Then she addressed Linda and Michael. "Come on, you two. I'm not going to bite you. I heard your story. You're in the clear.

"I thought I'd call your friends, the Smiths, because this morning a letter came from your mother addressed to Michael. The return address was a sanitarium. It seemed rather strange. The Smiths didn't answer. I was about to call the police or the FBI, and even read Michael's letter, when I got a call from your ranger friend. He gave me a brief outline of what's been going on. Don't stand here any longer. Come on in before your Uncle Cecil shows up again. He's been here twice today. It's a good thing he didn't locate you. He has some very queer ideas about taking you children home with him. You're here and safe. He can't do anything."

Even though Michael was 12, he hugged her right along with Linda. The twins came from behind and grabbed her around the waist. "I'm between, and you're choking me," Betty squealed.

Grandma squeezed each one of them. "All right, my dears, let's go into the house. Dinner is ready. It's late, but the ranger said it would be about this time. After you eat, we'll read the letter Michael got from your mother."

The children washed, combed, and made themselves quite neat. Then they went into the large farm kitchen, where they sat down to the long table with all kinds of good things on it to eat. It was the first table they had eaten from for over a week. Grandma filled their plates with vegetarian roast, potatoes and gravy, peas, and fresh vegetable salad. The children kept a large dish of biscuits going around the table, and she put more on the plate as soon as it was empty.

Joe glanced over the counter top and saw two beautiful pies. "Um, I won't be able to eat pie if I eat any more of this good dinner," he complained.

Grandma laughed. "Don't worry, Joe. The pie will keep." In the end they decided to save the pie for later. They wanted to hear their mother's letter.

As they filed into the living room they discussed what a wonderful dinner they had enjoyed. "It's nice not to have a picnic, isn't it, Linda?" Betty asked.

"It's wonderful," she replied.

When they sat down, Grandma said, "I don't feel like lecturing people when they're hungry. It won't do any good when they're full. In this case, as I said, I'd been frightened to death and warned and explained to before you arrived. I don't suppose the same circumstances will ever come up again. I know you meant well. You didn't want to worry your mother, and you didn't want to waste my money. You didn't want to argue with your Uncle Cecil. After this, trust me more and tell me your troubles. We're all one family. Will you do that?"

"We will," the children agreed.

"We'll tell you everything," Betty added.

"It's the best way," Grandma advised. "Then we can

work things out together, with God's help."

Michael and Linda smiled at each other in relief, and he said, "I'm happy. I'm through being head of the family. It's hard to tell people what to do when you're not sure yourself."

"I'm glad I'm not the mother," Linda said. "Sometimes I didn't feel like doing what I knew Mom would do. I need Mom to instruct me. We're not old enough to decide everything for ourselves."

Michael looked up as she finished.

"Well," his grandmother said, "it seems your mother is being well taken care of. She has the same trouble you children have had. If she'd told me some of her problems long ago, we could have straightened them out together, but we can begin now.

"There's a lot in her letter about a radio a gentleman from Cheqasa left at the sanitarium for her. She says it will help her pass the time while she's away from her family. Naturally she's very curious about who sent it. I imagine you can shed some light on the mystery in your next letter to her."

They laughed, and Michael asked, "Do you know about that, Grandma?"

"The ranger told me. We'll have to start getting ready for your mother to come home. I know it won't be long."

"This is a happy Sabbath, Grandma," Linda said. "I'm so glad we got here before sundown."

Grandma squeezed Linda's hand. "We have many things to be thankful for. This house will ring with praises and thanksgiving."

"The angel guards watched over us," Betty whispered softly, for she was nearly asleep.